# THE RACE OF RACES

© 2015, 2019 Randolph Walker, Jr.
Cover Image © 2016 Randolph Walker, Jr.

10 9 8 7 6 5 4 3

ISBN 9781020001123

45 Alternate Press, LLC
Hampton, Virginia

# THE RACE OF RACES

## A NOVEL OF SOUTHERN POLITICS

### RAN WALKER

# CONTENTS

PART THREE
KEITH LAWRENCE

# PART ONE

## DAVID MCKLUSKY

## CHAPTER ONE

DAVID MCKLUSKY LOVED HIS DAUGHTER, but he hated his wife. It hadn't always been that way, though. At one point, he had earnestly believed his wife, Bethany, was the most amazing woman he had ever met. She was intelligent and witty, and in the early years of their college courtship, she had been full of a sexual vigor that rivaled adult movie stars. It didn't hurt that she was also the niece of Billy Stamps, the owner of Stamps Plastic Works and one of the wealthiest men in Mississippi.

During the timeline of the seventeen years of their marriage, David found it difficult to discern exactly when that love had become apathy and that apathy had become outright disgust. Bethany had, however, given birth to his only daughter, and that alone was worth working to salvage their marriage, he supposed. Even more, he was determined to prove to Billy Stamps that he was not a duplicitous man who had, like a number of other men who enjoyed membership at the local country club, "fucked his way into wealth."

Those seventeen years had taken quite a toll on him, as they had her, and although both David and

Bethany had expected change, neither expected it to the degree it had actually occurred. David had come to realize politics was his true calling, and Bethany had come to realize she was far less tolerant of the growing racial imbalance in the county.

As a white lawyer in a small Southern town, David had a number of black clients, and he viewed his relationship with the black community in Daily as being favorable—as it would need to be for him to be successful as a politician. That was the primary reason he was taken aback when Bethany mentioned, over breakfast one morning, that she wanted to pull Heidi out of Daily High School, now that the summer break had begun, and enroll her in the private, all-white Adams Academy.

"What's wrong with Daily High?" David asked. "She's doing well—and her grades are pretty good."

"I can't see how you'd want your daughter around all of those thugs and babies' mamas."

"They're not all thugs and babies' mamas, Bethany."

"But a lot of them are. You can't stand there and tell me that blacks don't like drugs and sex. They can't help it. It's in their DNA. And since Heidi is about to start applying to college, I think she'd have a better application if she graduated from a more *respectable* school."

David sighed, irked even more by his wife's emphasis on the word "respectable," a word she delivered in a grating manner more Southern than even a Mississippian could bear. He hated when she got on her racist rants, but he figured her ramblings were largely harmless as she only seemed to do them in the comfort of their home. "I think Heidi'll be fine where she is now," he responded.

"That's just not a gamble I'm willing to take."

David sighed, barely concealing his growing exasperation. He tried his best to avoid these types of conversations, only because he knew ultimately he would be vilified for failing to toe the more conservative line of his in-laws. He finally asked, "Well, what does *Heidi* want?"

Bethany's eyes widened and her chest puffed out a bit making her look like a blowfish. "*We're* the parents, David," she said, whining his name, something she enjoyed doing when she wanted him to feel stupid for disagreeing with her. "*She's* the child. We know what's better for her than she does. It's *our* responsibility to step in on matters like these."

"Do you think it would be wise to ignore her wishes? After all, she *is* sixteen. Surely, her opinion has to have some value."

"Well, okay. If it makes you happy, I'll ask her what she thinks," Bethany huffed. "But if she agrees to transfer from Daily High to Adams Academy, then do you agree to sign off on it?"

David knew this was a battle he would eventually have to concede, but he wanted to make sure his wife understood that there was at least a semblance of backbone somewhere in the flesh he called his body.

"I'm just a little worried about the election," he offered. "This new senatorial district cuts through a lot of black communities, and moving Heidi to Adams, especially right now in the summer before the primary, might cost me quite a few votes. I would hate for black people to take Heidi's move as a personal slight against them."

Bethany laughed, slapping her hand firmly on the table in front of him. "I can tell you three reasons why you'll still win that election, especially if you only have to run against that black girl, Chante House. One, you're a good Christian man; two, you're good at raising money, *real* money; and three, just about everyone in the county with a lick of sense knows that blacks don't like to vote. With a little luck, it might even rain on election day."

## CHAPTER TWO

"DAVE, it would probably be better, politically speaking, to let Heidi start the school year at Adams Academy, if you and Bethany decide to take her out of Daily High," said Gasper Tate, between bites of his Caesar salad.

The two men sat across from each other in one of the booths in the back of The Wagon Train Diner, the dim lights providing them an added level of privacy. David's brow furrowed as he considered Gasper's words. "As my campaign manager, that's the best advice you have?"

"I sense that's not what you were expecting me to say."

"I don't know what I was expecting," David responded. "Maybe I'm just too close to this thing, but I can't imagine carrying enough votes to win this election if I'm claiming to represent a district that's roughly sixty percent black and I pull my daughter out of the only school that has black students."

Gasper took a sip of water and placed the glass down next to his plate. "Hell, Dave, you know me. I think Daily High is probably a better fit for her, but it's not about how *I* think; it's about how your wife thinks —and how her family thinks. And just in case you forgot, they have an enormous amount of power and influence throughout this part of the state. So if you end up having to move Heidi to Adams Academy—and let's be serious, you probably will—then you'd want to put it out there and control the spin immediately. You could say that she didn't have access to a lot of those classical subjects like Latin and whatever the hell private school kids are studying these days. That would beat getting the black vote and then turning around and shafting them by pulling her out of Daily High later. At least people can respect you for not looking like you're doing it behind their backs."

David chewed lightly on the inside of his cheek, a habit his dentist had warned him against doing, but when his nerves began to stir, he couldn't help it. "I'm actually hoping that Heidi will shoot all of this down so we don't have to go through with it."

Gasper chuckled, the red whiskers of his bearded chin bouncing up and down. "I'm sure there are frogs out there wishing for wings so they don't bump their asses every time they hop."

At this, David allowed himself to smile.

"There's also another way of going about his," Gasper said.

"I'm listening."

"We need to call in all the favors you're owed by any of the black men in the community, particularly the preachers. Show them the real you. Put that goodwill to use. Most married men know they'll have to make some major concessions to their wives, so behind closed doors, at least, you can make Heidi's transfer look like it was all Bethany's idea—which it is."

"I can't throw her under the bus like that. You know I'd never hear the end of it from Billy Stamps."

"You're not throwing her under the bus. You're just sharing an inside joke with other married men. I can't think of a single married man who hasn't been forced by his wife to do something he didn't want to do."

"I wouldn't look too weak?"

"If you're weak, then we're all weak," Gasper said.

That was easy for him to say, David mused. Gasper's wife had died from cancer three years earlier and he was now a millionaire, free and clear of her family. The only thing Gasper had to do now was not remarry, keep his indiscretions private, and not slip up and mention to anyone just how much he had hated his wife to begin with.

"So be honest here. Do I really have a chance of winning this race, or am I setting myself up for defeat?"

Gasper shrugged his shoulders. "I can't really say, Dave. I guess it's just like they always say, 'There're only two ways to run for public office: unopposed and scared shitless.' I would say we fall in the latter category."

# CHAPTER THREE

DAVID SAT in his law office with the door closed, reviewing precinct information Gasper had cobbled together for him. Because the district was new, there was nothing that was one hundred percent accurate about how the precinct turnouts would operate. District 44 was the result of the state legislature's latest attempts at gerrymandering to improve diversity in the Senate, a move that was met with a great deal of scorn by many of the senators in Jackson, some of whom claimed outright that it was an affirmative action seat and that whoever was elected from District 44 would find himself damn near blacklisted in terms of the better committee assignments. Much of this thinking was the result of rumblings from the white male majority in the senate, according to Gasper. Gasper assured David that such an ostracizing mark would not apply to him, though, because another white man in the state senate was hardly a threat. In fact, Gasper added, many whites would see David's being elected as having the added bonus of filling the seat for the newly redistricted area, while keeping the number of minorities (which, in

Mississippi, meant black people) to a minimum in the Senate.

While many senate districts tended to encompass several counties, District 44 was primarily on the western part of Humma County, with at least seventy percent of the constituents coming from that area. Another fifteen percent came from an adjacent county referred to by both black people and white people as Brown Sugar County, although the county was officially named Boxun. (David could not count on that county to produce a lot of votes because ninety percent of their locally elected politicians were black.) The final fifteen percent was cobbled together from a rural area in the northern portion of Mudbone County. People there were black, white, and Hispanic, and while one would think there would be a diversity of political ideology, given the demographics, they tended to vote as a uniform block. In fact, among some of David's in-laws, he had heard Mudbone County referred to as a haven of niggers, white niggers, and Spanish-speaking niggers. Clearly, if David were to win this election, he would need to take the majority of the votes in Humma County and put in some work in Mudbone to shore up their support as well, in hopes of angling them in his direction.

The greatest irony of them all, however, was that David considered himself, in his heart of hearts, to be a Republican. In Humma County, however, no politically-inclined white person would ever admit to being a Republican, primarily because the county, anchored by Daily, was famously and historically Democrat. As a result, the primary elections were the only elections that really mattered, because no one ran on the Republican ticket. Thanks to Nixon-era Republican efforts to re-characterize the Democratic party using the

"Southern Strategy," it had become the only political party a black person could vote for while maintaining any degree of loyalty to the civil rights movement, which had been big in Daily during the sixties. And because black people composed a slight majority in the county, white politicians could not alienate those votes by running for office as a part of a political party black people would never vote for. As a result, the town, at least on paper, was 99 percent Democrat. When it came to gubernatorial races, though, a sizable portion of the white population of Humma County were proud supporters of the Republican candidate. This charade of racial politics fooled no one, but it was still important to play the game, because even though one's true party affiliations were part of the statistical data of the state wide polling services, no one wanted to be caught with his or her pants down by offending this population of the local electorate.

Ever since he went down to Humma County Courthouse and declared himself a candidate for the senate seat, David had been privately questioning the wisdom of his choice. This was, after all, his first time running for public office, although he had served an appointed stint as City Attorney for Daily a few years back. Being appointed was nice, but he privately relished the thought of being an *elected* official. He hated to admit it, but the idea of public service excited him more than the deep six-figure salary he made at his law firm, a salary that did not include bonuses. In fact, he had taken home just under two million last year, mainly because of his firm's limited representation of businesses like Stamps Plastic Works, First National Bank, and a handful of carefully picked, and therefore settled, personal injury cases that were funneled to him through larger out-of-state firms looking to involve local counsel.

Despite his apparent financial success, David did not consider himself a trial lawyer in the truest sense of the words. He did not see himself as altruistic either. What fascinated him the most about the arena of state politics was that he had the ability to affect change. What kind of change? He was not entirely sure at this point, but he enjoyed the idea that he would be in the room helping to make the decisions when the big issues of the state presented themselves. Such a legacy would hopefully push him out from under the enormous, looming shadow of his wife's family name and allow him to be evaluated independently, on his own merits—or so he hoped.

Gasper had supplied the numbers of registered voters to all of the precincts in question, along with the percentage of people who had voted in the last ten elections. Beneath those pages was another stack of pages, including the names of all of the registered voters in those precincts. Gasper's strategy for pulling out the vote was a carefully constructed grid of precincts that he felt could lead to a political victory, but in order for that to happen, they would have to call in an overwhelming number of favors that, up to that point in Humma County politics, had no precedent. And when one considered the historical nature of the campaign, in that there was a black candidate in every single race on the Democratic ticket, there would need to be a financial incentive for the leaders of certain communities to offer their loyalty. Gasper viewed this act as not "buying votes," but, instead, stimulating enthusiasm for David's candidacy by offering transportation funds for those who would carry voters to the polls on election day, as well as other creatively repurposed funds.

David wiped his forehead and reached into his coat pocket, pulling out the third of his three cell phones (the other two being his personal and work phones). This was the phone that only one other person knew about. It was also a "Go" phone and not capable of being tracked via a cell phone bill. Even Gasper had no idea this phone existed.

David punched the "one" key to dial the preprogrammed number and held the phone to his ear.

"Hi."

"I really need to see you today," David said.

"Sure. What time did you wanna get together."

Her voice moved over him in soft, easy waves, and for a moment he thought about telling her that he loved her, which he did, but he wasn't ready to tell her yet, even after a blissful six months.

"I can get away this afternoon for a few hours. I'll call you back in an hour."

"Okay. But are you all right? I can hear the stress in your voice."

"It's just one of those days."

"Well, I have something to help out with that," she responded.

He chuckled softly into the phone. "You always know what to say to make me smile."

"That's because I know my man. I'll make sure that you have a much better day, okay? So try to relax in the meantime. Do that for me."

"I will."

"See you soon?"

"Definitely."

David put down the phone, and for the first time all day, he felt his mood lighten.

# CHAPTER FOUR

DAVID LAY ACROSS THE BED, naked, sweat pooling around his chest and along the slight grooves along his sides. He knew he needed to take off those extra twenty-five pounds but had yet to get around to it. He stroked the thin arm draped across his chest. Together, he and the equally soaked woman lying next to him looked like a double-tube crazy straw. Even as his exhausted chest rose and fell, he could feel his body glowing, an amorous swell filling him from head to toe.

"You feel better?" she asked, nestling her curly hair in the nook of his shoulder.

He hummed in response, his voice a brilliant and resonant baritone that caused her to smile.

"I love it when you do that. I can feel your chest vibrating against my face."

He smiled, allowing his fingertips to dance through the curls of her hair. The texture was thicker and heavier than Bethany's, but it was comforting in a way he could not readily articulate.

"Erin, Erin, Erin," he sang playfully, still basking in

the glow of their lovemaking. "I don't know what I would do without you."

"Really?" she asked, smiling and placing a kiss on his chest.

David found himself always on the edge of saying far too much when he was with her. "I'm just saying that I think about you all the time."

"I think about you, too," she said, sitting up and looping her arms around her knees. "I just don't see why you don't go ahead and tell her about me. Then we could move in together."

David shook his head. This was the only thing about Erin that bothered him: she didn't seem to grasp the nature of the situation he found himself in or the cast of players who were involved in defining what his life in Daily had become. "You know we can't do that. At least not yet."

"We could leave Mississippi and go to some island somewhere and live on a beach and make love under the sun."

David smiled, considering this. "I love the way that sounds. Really, I do. But you know I'm running for office over in Humma County, and there're so many factors at work right now. I have a daughter who'll be graduating next year and going off to college. Just give me a little more time."

Erin laughed and rose from the bed.

"An island, you say?" he repeated.

"Yeah. And you're changing the subject."

David smiled. "Never that."

Erin smiled in return and nestled herself in the crook of his arm again.

David wrapped his arm around her and glanced down at her smooth brown skin. "You're beautiful," he said, tracing his finger along her arm. She placed a light kiss on his chest, and the feeling of her hair tickled his chin.

"You're not so bad yourself."

Just then the words eased up his throat and rested just behind his teeth. If he said another word to her, it would be that he loved her.

"I just wish I could vote for you," Erin said, interrupting his thoughts.

"It's probably better that you live outside the district because I would be too distracted."

Erin rolled her eyes playfully. "Sure you will."

He chuckled nervously. Having her that close would be dangerous for both of them. The fact that he had to drive forty-five miles to get to her was a good thing.

He had, against his better judgment, fallen in love with her, and he knew a scandal of this magnitude would destroy his family if it ever came to light. Still, he was too far gone, because, with Erin, he felt something that made him come alive, something that made this duality a necessity to his life.

He didn't know how all of this would resolve itself —or if it ever would—but his plan was to win the election, see his daughter graduate from high school, and build up a nest egg, just in case things with Bethany did not work out over the next few years.

## CHAPTER FIVE

GASPER WAS successful in setting up meetings with several black pastors in the community, and David had gone through and given his pitch for their support. At first they were reticent about whom they would support, several of them even offering up tentative support for Chante House, the young black attorney who was also running for the senate seat. David understood their inclination to support his opponent, and he wasn't expecting all of them to come around, but he was hoping that a few of them might break rank.

After an afternoon of driving around the county meeting with pastors from different precincts, David found only one pastor willing to speak to his congregation on David's behalf, and that was only after David offered him a sizable contribution to his upcoming pastor appreciation day.

"Well, at least you got one to go on record for you right now," Gasper mused, as they sat in David's office, recovering from their afternoon meetings.

"Yeah, I got one. But did I get the *right* one."

"If it's any consolation, we'll probably have greater inroads with other community leaders in the precincts.

From what I hear, the influence the ministers carry these days isn't what it used to be anyway."

"Let's hope so."

"Well, we're pulling in donations from your white constituents, all ten of them," Gasper joked.

David shook his head, exasperated. He had questioned whether even running for this particular office was worth the effort, but like many a politician, he had been told by certain people close to him that he could count on their support, should he decide to run. A number of them were black lawyers and law enforcement who felt that Chante House had not paid her dues to the community, having just moved to the county not even a year earlier and already throwing her hat in the ring for a political position. They had told him they would support him, but that they couldn't do so publicly, as the illusion of racial solidarity affected their jobs as well.

David understood all of this, but was surprised at how little traction he was making publicly against a woman whom he bested in experience by nearly two decades. He also knew he could outspend her at every turn, but he would be counting on donations from whites who weren't even in his senatorial district or, worse, spending his own money—something he was by now not totally against.

"The yard signs came in today," Gasper said. "I have a number of businesses lined up who will let you post signs along the main highway in front of their buildings."

"Good," David said. This was the first bit of good news he had heard all day.

"Hey, I tried to call you yesterday afternoon and couldn't get you."

"Oh, I was out running some errands."

"For *four* hours?"

"I had errands, Gasper."

Gasper shrugged his shoulders. "You know this isn't the first time you went off the grid on me. Is there anything I need to know?"

"What are you talking about?"

"I'm just saying. If there's something I need to know, for the sake of the campaign, I think you should tell me. After all, I'm not just your campaign manager. I'm you're friend."

"I swear there's nothing to worry about. I just stepped away from my phone. That's all."

Gasper nodded. "I'll take your word for it."

"You do that," David said, smiling. "Now let's get out there and round up some more votes."

## CHAPTER SIX

AS THE SUMMER WORE ON, Gasper's internal polling numbers showed that David had made significant inroads with the voters in Humma County. Because Chante House was single and had an openly gay campaign manager, speculation about her sexual orientation gradually began to circulate, and in the conservative Bible Belt of Northeast Mississippi, that proved to be problematic. Although she had spoken out against the rumors on a few occasions, albeit privately, the idea that she might be a lesbian was too juicy for people to ignore. David asked if Gasper had been the source of this rumor, but Gasper denied he had anything to do with it. Still, her loss was his gain. And while he disagreed with whether a candidate's sexual orientation should matter anyway, he kept his thoughts private. He was having a hard enough time keeping the race close to worry with fighting battles on behalf of his opponent. This was politics, and Chante House would have to figure out a solution to her own problem.

At home, however, David was losing the battle with Bethany over whether or not they would send

Heidi to Adams Academy. When he arrived home early one evening, Bethany was ecstatic beyond measure as she told him that Heidi had agreed to go to Adams. The decision sounded so unlike Heidi that David immediately walked upstairs to her room and asked if she had a few minutes to talk with her old man about what she had told her mother.

When he walked into Heidi's room, he realized it had been a while since he had actually been inside of it. Of course he stuck his head in the doorway every other night to check on her, but he hadn't walked in and felt the world of her room envelop him from every angle. He pulled up the chair at her desk, as she lay across her bed, a magazine spread open before her.

"So your mom says that you want to leave Daily High."

"Dad, I can't go back there."

"Why? What happened?"

"I just can't go back." She pretended to be engrossed in her magazine, and this annoyed him.

"Heidi, put the magazine away. I just want to talk."

She huffed, rolled her eyes, and continued reading.

He knew that if this had been him behaving this way toward his parents when he was her age, his father would have snatched the magazine away, but he couldn't allow himself to be that aggressive with Heidi. She was his only daughter, his princess, and he vowed when he and Bethany were finally able to bring her home from the neonatal intensive care unit that he would do everything he could to make sure that she never suffered any more than she had during those first two months of her life.

"If you ever want to talk about what happened, I hope you know that you can come to me," he finally offered.

She nodded, not looking up from the magazine.

He rose to his feet and began walking toward the door. He started to turn around, but he didn't want to push the issue. She had clearly made her decision, and Bethany had won that fight. His job now was to adjust and keep things moving along.

As he reached the threshold of her bedroom doorway, he heard Heidi's voice. "Thanks, Dad."

"Sure thing," he responded, smiling at her, before turning to leave.

## CHAPTER SEVEN

GASPER HAD BEEN the first one to tell David of the rumor.

After Gasper traipsed around the information for a while, David finally pinned him down and got him to talk.

"I don't know if it's true or not, but I'm just letting you know what some people are saying. Especially since it concerns your daughter's boyfriend."

The accusation was odd indeed, but David was determined to maintain an unperturbed facade. "It just sounds too ridiculous to be true. Where are you getting your information?" he asked.

"Different people are starting to say this. Dave, it's got legs and it's making the rounds."

"Maybe Chante House's people are trying to get back at us because they think we had something to do with that lesbian rumor."

Gasper shook his head. "I don't think any blacks know about this one yet. This is being whispered strictly in certain quarters of privilege."

"Brent Edwards is adopted. I can buy that. But what I can't buy is that he's black," David said, struggling to piece it all together. "That kid is as WASPy as they come. If he were black, that would have come out a long time ago, especially in a community this small."

Gasper sighed. "When Mr. Edwards passed away last year, Mrs. Edwards broke down and told the boy that he was adopted."

"Seriously?"

"Yeah. I think she was trying to let him know that he had other family out there, since he was taking the loss so hard."

"So they tracked down the birth mother then?"

"Yeah. But she's white."

"So why are we having this conversation then?"

Gasper interlocked his fingers and rested them on his lap. "The word is that she gave the boy up for adoption because the father was black. I don't think she knew the baby would turn out looking as white as he did."

David leaned back in his chair. He wasn't quite sure he believed any of this. It was too absurd. But then he thought about how weird Heidi had acted when he asked her about why she wanted to transfer from Daily High. Did she know any of this? Was that why she wanted to attend Adams? After all, you couldn't get any farther from black people than going to a school like Adams.

David sat quietly for a moment considering the possibility that this young man, the one who had been dating his daughter for the past two years, this kid who was the star quarterback at Daily High, this kid who had been in his house numerous times and, God forbid, possibly shared intimate moments with his daughter, this *fucking* kid, had been passing for white all along. Or maybe he didn't know he was black at all. Who knew?

But none of that mattered now. David's fatherly instincts were kicking in strongly, and all he wanted to do was drive home and confront his daughter. Was she still dating him? Then he thought about Bethany and Billy Stamps and wondered if they had heard the rumor yet. If so, this situation was about to blow up quickly.

What would he do if what Gasper told him was true?

Gripping his steering wheel, he seethed, anger raining from his pores in waves. He couldn't identify the total source of his anger, but something about the situation had made his daughter vulnerable, and while a person could have attacked David directly in any way, to cause harm to his daughter was akin to signing your own death certificate.

## CHAPTER EIGHT

DAVID FOUND himself driving aimlessly around Daily, attempting to clear his head. When he and Bethany had decided to move to this small town seventeen years earlier, he had been the one pushing for Daily, not Bethany. She preferred a much closer proximity to Jackson, but he had become enamored with Daily after seeing pictures of it in a Sunday *Clarion-Ledger* newspaper profile. It looked like a hybrid of Norman Rockwell's small town America and what he imagined William Faulkner's Jefferson, the fictitious county seat of Yoknapatawpha County, to look like. He even liked the name Daily, because it suggested that type of beauty was not a sporadic occurrence, but a regular feature of the town's existence.

Daily was the seat of Humma County, a place that literally translated from Choctaw into "red," the color of the clay that could be found in various areas of the county, packed—or better yet, baked—into the Mississippi earth. The fact that there were no longer Choctaw people in the area (as they had been forced out nearly a century earlier) did not seem to discourage the white settlers from adopting the indigenous vocabulary.

Choctaw Chief Pushmataha's name still carried a currency in the area, if only with the local boy scout council, but it showed a willingness by the white citizens to celebrate the county's Choctaw heritage, although primarily for sport, as the closest Choctaw reservation was located just outside of Philadelphia, Mississippi, a place with its own dark civil rights history, one that included the murders of three voting rights activists in 1964.

Besides the beauty of the town, David wanted desperately to get away from Billy Stamps. If they had remained in Jackson, he would have surely been working for the old man. While there were probably things far worse than serving as general counsel to a plastics company, Billy Stamps was the kind of man who believed in micromanaging everything, both professional and personal. David saw this firsthand when Stamps Plastic Works was sued five years after David and Bethany had set up shop in Daily. David's firm was associated with Billy Stamps's Jackson firm and given the task of handling certain aspects of discovery, namely depositions that were being conducted in Daily by Grady Sails, a small-time black attorney who lucked up on two clients who just happened to live in Humma County.

It had been a Pyrrhic victory, but a victory nonetheless, and while Stamps Plastic Works took a major PR hit, the jury decided in its favor, leaving the plaintiffs with nothing but a sour taste in their mouths. The entire time, though, Billy Stamps had been overly involved, determined to leave as little to chance as possible. He even insisted on reading and correcting everything David worked on. That case could not have ended quickly enough for David, and he vowed that he would one day seek a way to carve out his own legacy, rather than spend his days protecting, whether directly or indirectly, another man's legacy.

As David drove down Main Street, he admired the repainted 5 cent Coca-Cola ads that had been stenciled onto the sides of several buildings decades earlier. The downtown area was still alive, unlike many of the other downtown areas throughout Mississippi that had the misfortune of having a new highway divert traffic away from their businesses. Daily was still holding on to that "small town" look that had originally attracted David.

He needed to see these things to clear his head and remind himself that he and Bethany had chosen this place for a reason. This was the place they would rear their daughter, a place where she would be protected and loved and given the chance to blossom into a beautiful young woman without the persistent intrusions of Billy Stamps. Heidi was the best thing about David, the one thing in his life that was not imbrued with some past sin, and to him that was perfection. So how dare that Edwards kid sully that perfection?

The anger began to rise in him again and wipe away the solace of his drive. Now he wanted only to talk to his daughter.

Pulling into his driveway David could feel his third cell phone vibrating in his front pocket. He let it go to voicemail.

Erin would have to wait. He had more pressing things on his mind.

# CHAPTER NINE

DAVID WALKED into his house to find Bethany and Heidi seated across from each other at the dining room table. They appeared to be in the middle of a conversation, but that did not prevent David from pulling up a seat at the head of the table.

"What's going on?" he asked, wondering if either one of them would give him the proper respect of telling him the truth.

Bethany answered, almost too quickly, "We were just talking about the coming school year and college applications."

"Oh really," David responded. He paused, waiting for Bethany to say more, but she didn't. He turned to face Heidi. "So are you excited about Adams?"

Heidi's smile was fake, and it pained him to think his daughter had to pretend as if nothing was wrong, just to avoid hurting his feelings. "It should be a great senior year," she finally said.

"Let me ask you something then," David said. "Are you still dating the Edwards kid?"

Then he saw it: that momentary flash of fear, the one she would try to cover up with apathy, but fail. In that second, he had seen the truth of it all. Gasper had been right.

Bethany immediately spoke up. "They broke it off. You know how teenagers are."

"Is that true?" David asked, turning to face Heidi again.

She nodded solemnly. "It just wasn't working out. We were moving in different directions and decided that we needed to just make a clean break."

David nodded. "I see." He thought of saying more. He wanted to tell his family they didn't have to tip-toe around him. Looking at his daughter's face caused him to pause. "Well, maybe we could take the boat out on the lake this weekend. How does that sound?" he said, looking at Heidi, then Bethany.

"Okay, Dad," Heidi responded, as Bethany nodded her agreement.

"Well, all right then," he said, rising from the table. "I'm going to get a shower and lie down. It's been a long day."

As he walked upstairs, he expected to hear the voices of his daughter and wife, huddled in their hushed tones, continuing their discussion from earlier, but when he reached the top of the stairs, he realized that the two of them weren't quiet. They were silent.

## CHAPTER TEN

GASPER HAD good news for David when they met again. The campaign volunteers who had been canvassing various neighborhoods throughout the district were finding more people willing to take yard signs than they had originally expected. They were down to their last hundred signs, but Gasper was reluctant to order more.

"We don't want to do overkill on the yard signs. When you have too many of them out there, they start to blend in with the landscape and people ignore them. Plus, we need these last few for election day," Gasper said.

David found Gasper's strategy unusual, but credible, although he wondered aloud more than once whether holding that many yard signs for election day was wise.

"It's simple. You have a few of your volunteers holding signs across the street from the precinct. And the others we will use to plaster the district in the wee hours of election morning. When people wake up and head down to vote before work, your signs will be the first thing they see."

David had shrugged at the initial proposal. "Why not just put them all up now?"

"Think about what it was like as a kid to wake up on Christmas morning and see all of the presents under the tree that weren't there the night before. The day feels special when you go to sleep at night and wake up to such a dramatic change."

"I don't know. It just seems like it would be annoying to some people."

"Maybe," Gasper had responded, "but consider this: if they walked into their precinct to vote, which name do you think will have been most heavily reinforced before they mark their ballots?"

"You're assuming that they will still be undecided when they reach the polls."

"Until they mark the ballot, there is always the chance that they will vote for you, no matter how small that chance might be."

And that had settled it.

Whether it was due to radio and TV ads, the Facebook page Heidi had constructed for him, word of mouth, people who canvassed neighborhoods, existing signage, or some unknown factor, the fact was that a number of black households were now agreeing to post his signs in their yards, and that was a mark of significant progress.

If the work day had concluded with Gasper's news, David would have been a happy man—as happy as he could be, given the personal issues he continued to wrestle with at home—but then came the call shortly after Gasper left.

Billy Stamps.

Billy Stamps hadn't spoken to him since the previous Christmas, an event where he showered his only niece-once-removed, Heidi, with gifts normally reserved for a head of state. The gifts like computers, tablets, clothes, phones, and video games were left to David and Bethany, because Billy Stamps was giving gifts like ponies (really?), her first car, and even the deed to an apartment building in Madison, just outside of the capital city of Jackson. David had wanted to argue that such gifts were overkill for a sixteen-year-old girl, but Billy, determined to share his wealth with the only person representing the future of the Stamps clan, was going to do what he was going to do, without regard to opposition.

The call had been a short one.

"How is my favorite niece?" Billy started, clearly referring to Heidi, not Bethany.

David didn't know if Billy was fishing for information or if he actually knew something. David decided to feign ignorant, just to see what Uncle Billy knew, and responded, "She's just fine."

"I'm hearing things. Things that involve Heidi."

There it was, David thought. "What kinds of things?"

"Things," Billy said, pausing for dramatic effect, "things I shouldn't be hearing. I just want to know what you're gonna do about it."

David figured it was time to end this charade. He had been wondering how he would respond to the situation with the Edwards kid himself. Secretly he hoped everything would blow over. Heidi was already transferring and she had broken it off with the young man, so there wasn't a lot left to explore, as far as David was concerned. He explained this to Billy Stamps as clearly as he could, hoping that answer would satisfy the old man.

"You trying to tell me that ol' Jeb Truelove has got

more respect for the women in his family than you do?"

At that, David felt his blood turn ice cold and drain from his face. "I'm going to act like I didn't just hear you say that. Look, Heidi is my daughter, and I will take care of the situation. You hear me?" David's voice was on the verge of shaking, but he held it steady. He had never talked to Billy Stamps like that, but he knew the old man was out of control.

"You'd better take care of it, boy—or I will!"

The old man hung up on him, and David stared at the receiver for a full minute before placing it back onto the telephone's base.

He was still surprised that Billy Stamps had brought up Jeb Truelove. That backwards redneck was serving ten years over in Parchman for running over and killing a black kid earlier in the spring. The rumor was that the black kid had been secretly dating his niece. So it was clear that even though Billy Stamps was a respected businessman, he was not above the kind of old fashion justice popularly meted out in Mississippi prior to 1965.

David thought about Heidi and her sweet angelic face. She had grown up so quickly. It seemed like only last month that she was taking her first steps, saying her first words, declaring to her little friends how her daddy was the smartest man in the world. Now she was a woman.

Would he kill for her? Without a doubt.

Would he murder someone in cold blood, though?

Not if he could help it.

## CHAPTER ELEVEN

"I MISS YOU," he said, squeezing the cell phone against his ear. This was the first time he had spoken with Erin in over a week.

She sighed heavily. "What's going on, David?"

"I'm just dealing with some issues."

"Did I do something wrong?"

"You didn't do anything. I'm just going through some things."

"Things like what?"

"I can't really say."

Erin was silent for a moment, and David could tell that she was stewing at his secrecy. He had never been this way with her before, and she was not responding well to this new type of treatment.

"You don't want me anymore," she finally said and began sobbing into the phone.

"It's not that. Please don't cry."

"I'm sorry," she said, trying to hold it together, her jagged, pained breaths coming between each word.

"Can I see you?" he finally said. He had not really thought it through much, but he was at a point where he needed to do damage control if he were to hold on to this woman he so desperately loved. He didn't want to lose her any more than he wanted his daughter to suffer the humiliation of having to change schools because she had inadvertently found herself in an interracial relationship. "I'm leaving out in a few minutes. I will meet you at your apartment. Just please stop crying. I hate to hear you crying."

"Okay. I need to see you, baby," she uttered, her voice beginning to stabilize.

"Well, I'm getting my jacket, and I'll be on the road in a few minutes."

"All right, David. I love you."

"I love you, too," he responded, without even thinking.

He hung up the phone, realizing that he had finally said *those* words, the ones he had wrestled to conceal over the past few months. They had slid out of him so easily, so effortlessly.

He truly missed her, so he knew they had some major making up to do when he got there.

## CHAPTER TWELVE

AS DAVID EXITED DAILY, headed down the highway, away from the businesses and subdivisions that
filled the town's corridor, he could feel his stomach
knotting. He didn't know what he would say when he
saw Erin. He had yet to resolve whether he would tell
her everything or just enough to satisfy her curiosity.

The houses along the highway were spread out by
nearly one hundred yards each, with soy, cotton, and
corn fields interspersed between them. There was even
the occasional abandoned shack with an outhouse in
the back on the verge of collapsing beneath the weight
of stray vegetation. David imagined a time when those
houses were thriving homes, when children probably
ran across the porch waiving sticks at each other like
swords. He didn't know what had happened to the
people who used to live there, whether they were dead
or alive, or even if they had migrated into the county
seat, Daily. All that was left were these sparse shells,
like distant punctuation marks along the plain
landscape.

He had never wanted for much in his life, even as a
child. His parents were middle class and reared him as

such. Outhouses and cotton fields were things that he was aware of, only because he had been driven past them, not because he had ever set foot on them. He wondered if Erin had grown up with similar privileges.

He was still amazed at the randomness of how they had met. He had happened to be in an office supply store picking up an external hard drive for his home computer when he heard a voice say, "I wouldn't get that one. A lot of people complain about those drives. This one might be better." Erin then handed him a more sleekly packaged 1TB external hard drive. She pointed to the specifications on the side, but he could hardly pay attention to any of that, as he was dumbfounded by her beauty. He had never seen a woman that beautiful, while simultaneously being that close to her. Sadly, he had never even imaged beauty to be a prerequisite for a relationship, but when he saw Erin Yates for the first time, it were as if his world of drab black and white visuals had snapped alive with bold, brilliant hues, an electric technicolor explosion.

He was already bored with Bethany but had never felt compelled to act on it until he met Erin. Convincing her to go out with him was not as difficult as he had expected either, although when she learned of his marriage, she was reluctant to be anything other than his friend.

Persistence had worn her down, that and the fact that she found him fun to be around. That was all six months ago. They were still in the honeymoon stage of their relationship, he knew, but there were no signs of things letting up. The sex was still fresh and exciting, and he had taken to reading up on different sexual moves to impress her. He struck pay dirt when he started exploring tantric sex, and Erin told him that she had never experienced that kind of intense intimacy. In fact, their sex life had become so robust that he had gone from having sex with Bethany once every other month to not even bothering to have sex with her at all. He doubted his wife would divorce him for sexual abandonment anyway. It was not like she clamored for him. In fact, he did not rule out that she might have another lover on the side. Still, he didn't care.

Erin was the only one he cared about, and he had decided that he would at least be sexually monogamous with her if he couldn't be with her completely. That's what made the dilemma of telling her about his daughter's situation more grating. He knew he should be straight forward, but up until that moment, he had successfully avoided burdening Erin with any of his family life.

In his rearview mirror, miles of bare highway shot behind him; in front of him, miles of bare highway lay awaiting him. He sensed there was a metaphor about his life somewhere in there, but he didn't know exactly where it was. Sadly, it all looked the same to him as he pressed on.

## CHAPTER THIRTEEN

THE MOMENT DAVID walked into Erin's house, she embraced him with such force that she nearly knocked him down. He held onto her and kissed her so deeply his head began to swim.

They stripped themselves naked and made love in the foyer, just inches from the front door, their bodies sliding and pushing along the hardwood floor, seeking a friction that gave way with their perspiration.

Erin climbed atop him and, as she moved her hips rhythmically above his, whispered, "I love you so much." Her face was so close to his that the exhalation of her breath streamed through the inner canal of his ear. The sensation tickled him and he smiled, rubbing his fingers down the center of her back.

"I love *you*," he said, beginning to feel the freedom those words afforded him.

She stopped for a moment and looked directly into his eyes. "I can't tell you how long I've been waiting for you to say those words."

"I can't tell you how long I've been wanting to say them."

She leaned down and kissed him, and they continued making love as if it were the first time their bodies had ever touched, their flesh made new by the vocalization of their feelings.

Once they had climaxed in each other's arms, they lay side by side on their backs, their clothes disheveled and flung randomly about the floor.

"David, what's going on between us?" Erin said, panting, her eyes facing the ceiling, her arms out-stretched as her breasts rose and fell from exhaustion.

"We're good—as good as ever."

"But something was wrong before you came to see me. What happened?"

David sat up on the floor and faced her. "I'm just going through a few things with my daughter. That's all."

"You don't think that I'd understand because I don't have any children. Is that it?"

"Not at all. I wouldn't dare think that."

He was surprised that Erin mentioned her not having children. He thought it was too sore a subject to bring up so casually. They'd had a conversation about her ovarian cysts early in their relationship, and he knew she was sensitive about the "children" issue. She was unsure if she could ever have them, but the doctors had all but told her the risk wasn't worth it, so she'd quietly complied. She said that she was used to the idea that she would never be a biological mother, but David sensed that this was partially a cover for her true emotions. This was yet another reason why he rarely told her anything about his own daughter, other than the fact that he had one.

Still, hearing her bring it up in the manner she did made him feel obligated to finish telling her the truth. It was the least he could do, since they'd just emotionally exposed themselves to each other, pulling back the last curtain that shielded their vulnerabilities.

"We're taking Heidi out of public school and putting her in an all-white private school."

Erin's eyes widened. "Why would you do that?"

They rarely talked about race when they were together, knowing the obvious: he was white and she was black, so this conversation had the potential to be even more awkward than he had initially imagined.

"It was my wife's idea. But then my daughter signed on."

When Erin didn't respond, David continued. "There's a boy that she was dating."

"What about him?"

"Well, people believe he's black."

Erin shrugged her shoulders. "I don't get it. What do you mean?"

As he explained the story, it slowly dawned on him the irony of the situation: he was upset about his daughter dating a black guy, but he had no problem, not only dating, but falling in love with a black woman. The double standard of it all embarrassed him, and when he saw the look of disappointment in Erin's eyes, he dropped his head and stared at the floor.

"I can't tell whether you're upset because he's black or because you feel that he betrayed your daughter's trust."

David sighed. "I don't know. Maybe deep down I just don't want my daughter to get hurt."

"Hurt by whom?"

"Anyone. I don't want her feelings hurt by that Edwards kid or people talking behind her back or her family ostracizing her."

"But you're her family," Erin said. "Would you ostracize your own daughter?"

David shook his head and stood up. "I mean people like Billy Stamps and that clan. Every white person in Mississippi is not as open-minded as we would like to believe."

He thought about telling her what Billy Stamps expected him to do in response to all of this, but decided against it. There were only so many secrets you could share with a person at one time, even if you loved her.

"I'm not sure how to feel about this," Erin finally said, rising from the floor. "I thought I knew you, that with us race didn't matter, but now I'm not so sure."

"N-n-no," David stuttered. "What we have is beyond race."

"Are you sure? I mean, maybe the reason you won't leave your wife to be with me is because I'm black."

"I can't believe you just said that. You know me better than that. I love you, and we have a good thing. We do. And one day we *will* be together. You just have to be patient."

Erin began to walk toward her bedroom, and David followed. When she started the shower, he edged closer and wrapped his arms around her waist.

"I think I want to shower alone," she said, her voice so soft that he almost didn't hear her.

"What? What do you mean?" he said, reaching for her as she moved away from him.

"I don't know if I can trust what you say anymore."

"Oh come on," he said, exasperated. "We've been together long enough for you to know who I am. You can trust that I love you."

"Prove it."

"What do you want me to do?"

"I don't know. But you'll have to prove to me that what we have is real and worth something to you."

He leaned in to kiss her, in hopes that she could tell by the way he touched her that his feelings for her were true, but she turned away from him, stepped into the shower, and pulled the curtain closed behind her.

"Erin, come on."

"Maybe we need some time apart for you to figure out what it is that you want from this relationship," she said, over the drone of the water spraying behind the curtain.

"You're kicking me out?"

"No," she responded. "I'm just giving you a little time to think about things."

David stood outside of the shower, his erection a distant memory. His heart ached, and he wished so badly to be on the other side of the curtain, holding her in his arms, as the warm water sprayed against his back. He stood there for a moment, waiting. Surely she would open the curtain and invite him in if he were patient. But after five slow, agonizing minutes of silence, save the rush of the water, he turned around, dejected, and walked back into the foyer to retrieve his clothes.

Once he dressed, he paused in the threshold, the door resting against his shoulder, waiting for Erin's voice, for the water to stop, for anything that would signal to him that everything was all right, that they were all right. He was met with silence, so he retreated into the afternoon, closing the door quietly behind him.

## CHAPTER FOURTEEN

"YOU CAN REALLY WIN THIS THING!" Gasper shouted, unable to conceal his excitement. Normally any conversation that he and David had in The Wagon Train was done in hushed tones. Not today, though.

"Let's not get ahead of ourselves," David said, poking at the tuna salad on his plate.

"I thought you'd be happy to hear about the endorsements you picked up from those ministers we met with a while back. It seems like you have a third of them backing you right now. I would say that's a reason to be extremely optimistic."

"*Cautiously* optimistic," David said.

Gasper shrugged his shoulders. "Well, maybe you'll find this bit of news uplifting: from what I hear, Chante House's popularity is falling so fast, you would think that we tied a boulder to it and dropped it in the ocean."

David chuckled, never looking up from his plate.

"Dave, what's wrong? You've been acting funny all day. First, you don't answer your cell phone and then you have this strange attitude when you show up to work. Are you going to tell me what's going on or do I have to start guessing? I'm your best friend, and you're treating me like you don't trust me. Tell me something, Dave. Put my mind at ease. We have too much wrapped up in this campaign for you to be going off the reservation on me."

In that moment, David considered opening up to Gasper about Erin. Hell, Gasper was no saint. If anything he should have been able to appreciate David's desire to play the game that he himself had played. Of course Gasper would respond that he had remained married to his wife until death (did they part) and that he kept his side woman completely from view until well after the funeral, and somehow that odd contrast would be sufficient enough for him to turn up his nose at what David was doing.

No. He would not tell Gasper about Erin.

So he lied.

"This moving of Heidi from Daily High to Adams Academy has me a bit distracted." Truth be told, he had hardly given it any thought. After his conversation with Erin, he had decided he would do nothing more than what he had already done. The bottom line was that the Edwards kid was out of the picture (at Heidi's own doing) and she was on her way to Adams in the fall. What more was there to say on the matter? He figured that for the good of everyone involved, it was time to pretend that none of this had ever happened and to move on with life—and whatever damage control he would have to do when her school transfer became public.

Gasper nodded his affirmation. "I understand. But it's only for a year. Then she'll be in college, and all of this other stuff will blow over and be a distant memory."

"Maybe." David took a bite of his tuna salad.

"Trust me. If you have anything to worry about with Heidi, it's where you should send her for college."

"She wants to go to school out of state now. That's the latest. Before that she had been considering Ole Miss. But now all she's talking about is Texas A & M and the University of Tennessee." David almost let it slip that those schools had only become options after she had decided to transfer to Adams, but he held on to that bit of information.

"Well, at least she'll still be in the same athletic conference playing against Mississippi State and Ole Miss. Great SEC football either way," Gasper said.

David chuckled nervously under his breath. "Yeah, you're right."

Gasper reached over and patted him on the arm. "Buck up, Dave. We're in the home stretch now. Only three weeks until the election."

David allowed himself to smile. He would be glad when the election was over. The process had been a long and trying one, and while he had originally dug into it, focused on his appetite for constructing his own identity and legacy, his personal life had risen like a tsunami and threatened to drown him where he stood.

Almost as if on cue, his primary cell phone rang. He glanced at the display, and when he saw it was Billy Stamps, he let it go straight to voicemail.

David placed his napkin on the plate in front of him. "I'm going to need to go and take care of a few things. I'll call you a little later."

"No problem," Gasper said. "Make sure you give my best to Beth and Heidi."

David could only nod.

He reached into his wallet and pulled out a fifty dollar bill, placing it on the table.

"This should cover lunch," he said.

"Lunch *and* some," Gasper laughed.

David nodded and walked away, his thoughts propelling him toward an uncertain destination.

## CHAPTER FIFTEEN

DAVID HOPPED in his car and started out toward the western part of Humma County. The lush greenery of the hills and trees that lined the road reminded him of why he loved this part of Mississippi. The land was not as flat as it was in the Delta or as heavily populated as it was in the South-Central part of the state. It was not touchable by hurricanes, unlike the Gulf Coast.

He turned onto a side road and noticed a precinct building up ahead, on the left side of the road. This was the Waltilly precinct, located in his senatorial district. In three weeks people would be lining up at this precinct to cast their votes for the first senator of the 44th district. He hoped like hell that the majority of the votes cast here in this small community, roughly half black and half white, would go towards his candidacy. But the ferocity with which he had once wished this was not there anymore.

David pulled into the parking lot of the empty precinct and looked at his phone. There was a voicemail from Billy Stamps waiting for him. Since he had done absolutely nothing since the last time the old man had called, he knew he was bound to have his ass chewed up and handed to him as soon as the old man could get him on the line.

Staring at the small white brick building in front of him, David lifted the cell phone to his ear.

"If you're gonna drag your damn feet on this, I can make other arrangements."

That was it.

The message was so short and cryptic David had to listen to it several more times.

Did Billy Stamps mean that he was going to put out a hit on the Edwards kid? Did he mean that he was going to take a different approach? Was the message maybe a not-so-clear slight on David? Maybe there was some other meaning embedded in there, but he could not tell. The only way to know for sure would be for him to return Billy's call. But Billy had not requested that his phone call be returned.

David felt as though he were getting orders from the don of a crime family and that he was duty-bound to uphold the honor of the family, a requirement that came along with the privileges from which he had already benefited.

He turned in the driveway and continued to drive around the countryside as he waited for Heidi to get home. Before he returned Billy Stamps's call, he needed to make sure he had all the facts from his daughter. He would see what he could do to call off the dogs and seek a more reasonable solution. After all, Billy Stamps had all of the markings of a reasonable man. Didn't he?

## CHAPTER SIXTEEN

BY THE TIME David made it home, Heidi's car was parked in the driveway. Bethany's car, however, was not. At least he would be able to talk to his daughter without any interference from his wife.

He found Heidi camped out on the couch in the great room. The TV was on some channel that was playing music videos.

"Heidi," he said, entering the room. "Gotta minute?"

David normally didn't make it home until around six or seven in the evening. With the amount of time Heidi had to herself, along with the enormous size of their house, he counted himself lucky that she was only watching music videos and not doing something more mischievous.

"Hey, Dad. Home already?"

"Oh, I left something here this morning and just came by to pick it up," he said.

She shrugged her shoulders and turned back toward the TV.

"I wanted to talk to you for a minute. Can you turn off the TV?"

She clicked the remote and the screen turned black. She turned to face him, her face doing a poor job of concealing how annoyed she was with the interruption. David knew he and Bethany had spoiled Heidi her entire life, so he couldn't blame her completely for the flippant way in which she behaved. Plus, she was a teenager, and they were supposed to be difficult. At least she wasn't doing drugs or getting pregnant, he reasoned.

"I want you to tell me the truth when I ask you this," he started, suddenly feeling strange that he had to actually ask his daughter not to lie to him. "Why did you decide to transfer to Adams Academy right now, especially when you're on the verge of graduating from Daily High?"

Her eyes widened at his directness, so he watched her more closely, looking to see if she would use this as an opportunity to start being evasive.

"I just wanted a change a scenery."

"Why?"

"What do you mean 'why'?" she asked, her eyes beginning to dart back and forth, wanting to roll themselves in apathy but unable to.

"Why, all of a sudden, do you need a change of scenery?"

"I don't know."

There it was, the most basic, indecisive answer a parent could expect from a teenager who was blocking him from knowing her true thoughts. He decided in that moment to be more direct. A lot more direct.

"Are you leaving Daily High School because of Brent Edwards?"

Her eyes were large like the faces of grandfather clocks. He half-expected her mouth to open and a little bird on a perch to emerge and cuckoo the changing of the hour.

"I know what they're saying, Heidi. You don't have to play dumb with me."

He didn't know what he expected his daughter to say in response, but when she broke down crying, her body heaving violently with emotion, he knew he had sorely miscalculated his approach. There were just so many things he didn't know about rearing a daughter, and everything looked like a potential land mine. This time, though, he had carelessly walked out into the field and detonated the motherload.

David walked over and placed an arm around Heidi. For a second he thought she might push him away, but instead she threw her face into his chest, sobbing loudly. He brushed her hair with his hands, shushing her softly while mumbling, "Everything will be all right."

Once she had finally settled down, Heidi told him about how she had found out from one of her friends that Brent might have been black. If school were in session, she feared everyone would know, if they hadn't heard about it already on some social networking site. She might have lasted one more year, that final year, at Daily High School, except for the fact that one of the white guys from her class jokingly called her a "nigger lover" one afternoon while she was out with friends having lunch. The weight of it all forced her to do something to avoid the pending persecution.

David wanted to tell her the flaw in her logic, that people at an all white school would be equally, if not more, brutal if they suspected the same thing of her that this other kid had. But he kept his mouth shut on this point. It was important that she felt that she was working on a solution to her own problem.

At first she had not known what to do, but then Bethany had come along with the proposition, which, to Heidi, must have looked like a lifesaver, so she grabbed and held on tightly.

And, yes, Bethany was aware of what was being said, so David figured that Billy Stamps's knowledge of the situation had come from her.

As he looked at Heidi, he felt her pain and confusion, the anger that ate away at her. She was too young to have these kinds of concerns. She had done nothing wrong. She was just trying to extricate herself from a situation that had fallen to pieces all around her.

"Heidi," he said, still brushing her hair, "I don't want you to worry about a thing. I will take care of all of this. Okay?"

He could feel her head nod against his chest—and that affirmation scared him, because he didn't know what he would be willing to do to bring peace to his daughter's life.

## CHAPTER SEVENTEEN

DAVID DIDN'T HAVE any more of an idea of what he would do about the situation than he did prior to speaking to Heidi, so he laid out his options: (1) do nothing, which at this point was looking a lot less likely, given the state of things; (2) support Heidi's move to Adams and do what he could to diplomatically smooth things over, something he was already having to do, although this choice felt insufficient in the larger scheme of things; (3) meet with the Edwards kid and see if any of this stuff was true and not just an overblown rumor, because if it was a misunderstanding, just maybe, as a lawyer, he could help get the cat back into the bag; or (4) do what Billy Stamps wanted, which was not even an option as far as he was concerned. He was not a criminal; he was a loving father.

As he sat in his home study, he poured himself a glass of eighteen-year-old scotch that he only sipped on rare occasions. He was not much of a drinker, socially or otherwise, but occasionally he needed a taste to steady his nerves. And now his nerves were so on edge he felt the need to pour himself a dry double off the top.

Once he finished his glass, he poured another, and before he realized it, he had polished off the bottle. The only other whiskeys he had in his mini bar were a fifth of Jack Daniels and a fifth of Crown Royal (a gift from the landscaper who took David's light-hearted compliment of the purple and gold velvet bag the guy was using to hold loose change as an invitation to get him a bottle for his collection). David opened one and then the other.

Before he realized it, he was drunk. He had not been drunk since before Heidi was born, so he could barely remember what it felt like to be off kilter. He could only feel his anger bubbling inside of him.

He logged on to his desktop and did a Google search of Brent Edwards. The kid was the starting quarterback for the high school football team, and no matter how David scrunched up his face and stared at the screen, he could see nothing about the kid that looked *black*. And that angered him even more.

David stood up too quickly from his chair and felt the room spin violently around him. He walked toward the door, determined to drive around until he found the Edwards kid.

Just as he reached for the door handle, his hand slipped and he collided with the cool wood of the door and slid down onto the floor, where the world suddenly went dark.

## CHAPTER EIGHTEEN

DAVID COULDN'T REMEMBER EXACTLY how he ended up in his bed when he awoke the next morning. His head felt as if a giant were squeezing it between two fingers. He was now embarrassed by the idea of his rambling around drunk the previous evening.

Neither Bethany nor Heidi was home. He figured Bethany was out shopping, as usual, and that Heidi had gone to read to swing bed patients at the hospital where she volunteered most mornings. (Gasper had encouraged him to use her in one of their campaign ads, but he had refused, wanting to avoid bringing attention to Heidi's service projects for fear that he would look too opportunistic; in his mind he had not yet graduated to exploiting his family for political gain).

He was alone in the cavernous house, and for a while he just walked around in his bathrobe, coping with his hangover. He couldn't, for the life of him, remember what had happened the previous night, only that he had been really upset and had drank a lot.

He walked into his study and began hunting around for his Go phone. He would've hated to have taken it out or had it ring in Bethany's presence, but he couldn't find it. He went through his pants from the previous day, his suit coat, the desk drawers in his study, and even his briefcase. Between the banging inside of his head and the hunger starting to build in his stomach, he considered maybe calling the phone from his house number, but he realized that he never memorized the phone number, and even if he had, he didn't want any traces of that number anywhere in the house. In that moment he prayed that Bethany had not confiscated the phone. Surely he had just misplaced it. The fact that he couldn't tell either way reaffirmed the fact that he might want to hold off on taking another drink for a while. Clearly, through all of these years, he had never learned to hold his liquor. (When he thought about it, he realized even when he was living his fraternity days at Ole Miss, he had never been good at holding his liquor, having once been told that he had streaked across the campus after a night of drinking too much beer.)

He would deal with the phone issue later. He was already running late for work, and while he didn't have to punch a clock, the kinds of businesses he represented frowned upon undisciplined professionals. If your operating hours were from nine until five, they expected you to be available during those hours, available meaning dressed for work with the mental faculties to go along with it.

David dragged himself to the shower in the master bedroom and tried to wash away the filthy way he felt. Even his skin ached with the remnants of hard alcohol. He lathered himself with body wash and bathed himself repeatedly until he felt the temperature of the water starting to cool. He then dried himself, furiously brushed his teeth and gargled mouthwash, and then dressed himself carefully so that he didn't sicken his stomach and throw up on his clothes.

After adjusting the Windsor knot on his tie and checking his appearance in the mirror (he didn't look his best, but he was presentable), he headed downstairs to his study to get his briefcase and check again for the Go phone.

By the time he reached the study, he could hear the chimes of the doorbell echoing throughout the house. His brow furrowed. He had no idea of who that could be, given that no one was usually here during this time of the day as far as he knew. Then he had a fleeting thought: maybe Bethany had been cheating with someone while he was away at work after all. He thought that notion would anger him, but it didn't. He actually kind of hoped she had started seeing someone on the side. It would make the divorce much easier, maybe even expedite the process.

David walked through the foyer to the front door, hoping that he would open it and find some surprised golf pro standing there, erection primed to go. He still had enough alcohol in his system to knock someone out, if need be, only because he needed the release, not because he felt the need to fight for the sanctity of his failing marriage.

When he opened the door, he was surprised to find Allan Kincaid, one of the detectives from the Daily Police Department. Allan had not come alone either. A team of four other officers stood behind him.

"Allan, what's this about? Did something happen to Bethany?" he asked. "Heidi?" Now fear was beginning to take hold of him. If anything happened to Heidi he didn't know what he would do.

"Hey, buddy," Allan said, his hand resting against his holstered Glock. At first David didn't notice, but when he did, he suddenly became aware that all of the officers' hands were in the same position. "We need to ask you a few questions, if you don't mind."

"Sure. But what's this about?"

Allan had been an acquaintance at the country club for several years, so this was totally out of character for him to show up unannounced at David's home. In fact, David could not ever remember a time where he hosted Allan Kincaid in his home.

"Where were you last night?"

"What do you mean?"

"What were you doing last night?"

David couldn't remember a thing from the previous night, but as his faculties began to sharpen, he realized that Allan and company were there for *him*.

"We're gonna need for you to come down to the station to answer a few questions. We don't have to do the sirens and lights and all of that, but we're going to need to have you come with us."

David looked out into the driveway at the three dark unmarked cars. "Am I under arrest for something?" he asked.

"Right now we just want to ask you some questions."

David tried as quickly as he could to make sense of what was going on, but was failing miserably. Finally, his legal thinking kicked in, and he said, "I'm going to call an attorney and have him meet me there."

"Suit yourself, although I don't know why you'd need an attorney. You're not under arrest."

"Let's just say that I would feel more comfortable having my attorney present if you're going to ask me anything."

Allan smirked, as if to say, "These fucking lawyers think they are so damned smart."

David called Gasper and gave him what little information he had and told Gasper to meet him at the police station. After hanging up, David noticed that Gasper hadn't sounded particularly surprised to be getting this kind of call, which unnerved him quite a bit.

"We can trust that you're not gonna try anything crazy, right?" Allan said. "We don't need to use the handcuffs, do we?"

"Only if I'm under arrest, which you have already said that I am not."

David locked the door to his house and followed the officers out to their cars.

## CHAPTER NINETEEN

WHEN THEY ARRIVED at the police station, David realized he was thankful he had taken the time to dress in a suit. He would at least look like he was there in a professional capacity if anyone were to see him going into the station.

Gasper was already standing in the waiting room area. "Allan," he said. "How's it going?"

"Seems we have a little situation on our hands."

David knew that Gasper and Allan had a much closer personal relationship than David and Allan did. That made him more thankful his best friend had come because Gasper would make sure he was treated fairly until they could iron out whatever confusion had brought him there in the first place.

"Yeah, so I hear," Gasper responded to Allan.

David shrugged his shoulders. "What situation are you talking about? If something happened to my family, you have to tell me."

Allan turned to face him. "You don't have any idea of why you're here?"

"Not a single notion of an idea," David responded.

"Do you know that boy Brent Edwards who played quarterback for Daily High?"

By now David's mind was sharpening very quickly. He replayed each word in his mind and realized that Allan had mentioned the word "played." It was the awkward past tense that jarred him. Suddenly he blurted out, "Did something happen to him?" Even as the words left his lips, he knew he had messed up.

"Bingo," Allan said. "He was killed in a hit and run last night, and we need to ask you a few questions about what you were doing last night."

Gasper leaned in. "If you're going to ask my client anything, we'll need to do this in a proper setting, not standing out here in the waiting room."

David's stomach churned violently, and as he walked forward through the security doors into the nerve center of the police station, he felt the vomit shoot up the back of his throat. His stomach heaved and he projected the contents of his dinner all over Allan's back.

"For God's sake," Allan groaned, attempting to look at his back but being unable to see it. He almost looked comical, like a dog chasing his tail, but David could barely observe this because he had fallen onto the floor and curled up in a fetal position.

"Someone get an EMT over here," Allan barked. "And find me a shirt!"

Gasper knelt down next to David. "You okay, Dave? You look pretty bad."

"What happened?" David whispered between clenched teeth. "Why am I here?"

Even in his ailing condition, he knew someone had to have brought up his name for him to be at the police station.

"The police got a tip to check you out."

Having a friend who spent a lot of time hanging out with cops had its benefits. It would help him to fill in the blanks that much faster.

"A tip from whom?"

Gasper shook his head, trying to cut off the conversation until they could have more privacy.

David tried again, the full urgency of his confusion manifesting itself through every part of his body. "Gasper, from whom?"

Gasper said, "You really don't know?"

"Please, man!"

Gasper sighed and leaned down close to David's ear while cops moved around him, making way for the EMT. "Heidi, Dave. Heidi."

CHAPTER TWENTY

ALTHOUGH DAVID HAD NOT WORKED on a criminal case in years, he was surprised by how slowly the hands of justice moved. His initial appearance in court left him both confused and angry. The judge, a person to whom David had made generous campaign contributions in the past, denied his bail.

"Because of Mr. McKlusky's wealth, we feel he might be a flight risk," Judge Thompson mumbled, as if delivering lines from a script.

"I'm being set up," David whispered to Gasper. "Someone wants me to take the fall for this."

"Not now," Gasper whispered back, nodding his head to indicate they were standing in open court.

David was returned to his cell, and while he sat on his bed staring at the cold, gray walls, he tried to determine if there was any way he could have possibly killed anyone without knowing it. There was the "intent" part to a crime like this, and his alcoholic blackout had to play a role in him not being in the right state of mind. Still, he didn't think he had been the one to murder the kid. That just wasn't something he could ever imagine himself doing.

Bethany came to visit him once, only to tell him that she was sickened by what he had done and that the shame he had caused her and Heidi was forcing them to move to Jackson and stay with Uncle Billy.

Seventeen years and at the first sign of trouble, Bethany was packing up and leaving. David was too deflated to even be angry. She clearly didn't love him. This was her exit, and rather than fight her on it, he would let her go. At least he knew where he stood. Billy Stamps had been trying to get her and Heidi under his control, and he had now succeeded. It didn't take a genius to realize that Billy Stamps had set him up. David hadn't played ball, so this was the punishment for going against the Stamps clan.

Of course there was no way he could prove it. Billy Stamps had probably greased every palm from Biloxi to Corinth, and there would be no way out for David at this point. How else could he explain the stilted way Judge Thompson had distanced himself in denying David's bail?

Was there really enough evidence to sustain the charges? He seriously doubted Heidi's declaration would be enough to keep him behind bars. At best, she was working under an assumption, something purely circumstantial. She *had* to be—unless she was in on it, too.

He didn't know who to trust at this point.

"Gasper," he said, when they met the following day. "I need to ask you something, and I need you to be completely honest with me."

"Sure thing," Gasper responded.

"Do you think I really did this?"

Gasper paused, looking David squarely in the eyes. "I want to believe that you didn't."

"Do you think I'm being set up?"

Gasper shrugged his shoulders. "It doesn't feel that way. I think they really believe you did it. Heidi is pretty credible. She gave a statement about how you were going on a rant about killing the Edwards kid the night he was killed. Even if you didn't do it, you have to admit that's a hell of a coincidence."

David lowered his head. "I didn't do it. I don't known how I can prove it, but I had nothing to do with that kid's death."

"Well, as far as I'm concerned, you're innocent until proven guilty. It's the prosecution's job to prove that you did it. The burden is not on us."

"Without bail, I'll go crazy in here waiting for my day in court. Do you think a jury will convict me?"

"I don't know what these people will do. I imagine they will need to have more than Heidi's testimony, though. It wasn't like she saw you do anything. Their case is not strong. Unless they found some way of connecting your car to the crime scene, I don't think they would have enough to get you convicted."

David sighed. "I never moved my car that night. Believe me. I was too drunk to walk straight, let alone drive."

"You were drunk?"

David nodded.

Gasper leaned in closer to David. "Let's keep that to ourselves for now, okay? That might work for us or against us, depending on the jury we get."

"Yeah."

Gasper collected his briefcase and stood up from the table in the meeting room.

"I need you to do one thing for me before you leave," David said.

"Sure. Anything."

"I need you to call someone and let her know that

I didn't do any of this. It's really important that she know that. And tell her that I love her."

Gasper nodded. "Sure thing. I can drop by the house and tell Bethany when I leave here. I hope she's still in town."

"It's not her, Gasper, and you damn well know it. Just do this for me, okay?"

"Sure thing, buddy," Gasper said, taking out a pen and notepad. He wrote down the name and number David called out to him.

"I might be a lot of things," David said, "but I'm not a murderer. You've got to get me out of here."

"I'll do my best," Gasper said. He reached over and placed a hand on David's shoulder.

"It would've been funny if we had actually won that election," David said.

"Yeah, that would've been something," Gasper said, nodding to his friend, before walking away.

David returned to his cell and lay down on his bed, facing the brick wall. He could feel the exhalations of his breath bouncing from the wall back onto his face. He was alone, and while that knowledge terrified him to his core, he felt a sense of relief in knowing who his real friends were.

If he ever made it out of there, he would never take his life for granted again.

PART TWO

CHANTE HOUSE

## CHAPTER TWENTY-ONE

CHANTE HOUSE HAD BARELY BEEN at Sails and Associates for six months when her senior partner, Grady Sails, asked her to consider running for senator of the newly created District 44. She had laughed when he first mentioned it. She didn't know him well enough to understand his sense of humor, so when she heard something that sounded blatantly absurd, she defaulted to laughter.

"I'm serious," he said, not at all offended by her response. It was as if he had expected it.

"The ink on my bar license is still wet," she said, laughing again. When she realized he wasn't laughing along with her, she sat up in her seat, attempting to digest his words. "I'm still learning how to practice law."

Grady smiled. "You'll be learning how to practice law for most of your career. There's always something new to learn, so at best you will be *practicing* to be better until you decide to retire."

"Maybe so," she said.

"And just so you know, the law in Mississippi doesn't require a senator to be a lawyer, so that's not even an issue."

"But why me?"

Grady sat back in his seat, placing his chubby fingers into a steeple formation. Even in this pensive position, he reminded Chante of a dressed-up version of Fred Sanford. They could have easily been brothers. Grady finally said, "I've been giving it some thought, and while I know you're new to Daily, I think this'd be a good thing for you."

"How? I'm gonna lose! No one knows who I am around here."

Grady seemed unfazed by her response. "One of the reasons people run for office is so people in the community can learn their names. You can think of it like advertising, if that makes sense."

"Then why not just put regular business ads on the radio or TV?"

"People need to get to know *you*." Grady rubbed at the gray stubble on his chin. "Chante, you ain't giving yourself enough credit here. You'd make a great senator."

"Why don't *you* run? You'd win easily!"

Grady chuckled. "Maybe ten years ago, but I'm getting up there in age, and I think this position needs to be held by a young person. But this isn't about me. It's about you and the golden opportunity that's sitting in your lap."

"I know there have to be a lot of other people in Daily who're eyeing this position," Chante said.

"Yeah, but none of them are *electable*. White people are gonna rally around one candidate, and black folks are gonna have ten different people running, splitting up the vote all kinds of ways so that none of them has a chance. And that seat was set up to produce a black senator, so that would be ironic as hell if we messed this one up for ourselves."

Chante shrugged her shoulders. "If we're gonna end up splitting the vote, then why should I run?"

Grady smiled again, as if he'd been anticipating this question as well. "I've been talking to a few folks around her, and we've agreed the best person to run against the white folks is an educated, young person who has a good head his shoulders and can learn on his feet."

The word "his" didn't escape Chante's attention. Having grown up over in Grenada, she was well aware of how conservative many of the people in Northern Mississippi were and doubted that most of them would vote for a black woman, especially with a position this large. She mentioned this to Grady, who responded with a myriad of names of elected officials throughout the state who were black women: mayors, county attorneys, members of the House of Representatives, and, yes, even state senators. "One day a black woman will be governor of this state, so I don't want you dismissing yourself from consideration based off of your gender or your race."

She felt humbled by his comments. She knew she was sounding scared, but she found it difficult not to be intimidated by the idea of running for a state senate seat. Only minutes earlier she had been at her desk working on a response to a Motion for Summary Judgment, and now she was sitting in her boss's office, allowing him to persuade her to become a politician, something she had never even considered doing at any point in her life up to that point. It all felt like it was too much, too soon.

Chante said, "I'm sure there's someone with more experience than I have who would be willing to step up and do this thing, someone who already has better name recognition and knows how to get elected in this area."

Grady finally placed his hands on his desk and leaned forward, closing the distance between the two of them. "Chante, I know you're nervous about all of this. I get that. Who wouldn't be? But you're selling yourself short. You have an opportunity to do something major. So what if it came when you least expected it? Martin Luther King, Jr. was twenty-six-years-old when he spearheaded the Montgomery Bus Boycott. You know why he got picked? He was from out of town. He brought a fresh perspective and had little to lose. And don't get me started on Barack Obama. Both of those men did what no one expected them to do, and they were successful at it. Even more, both of those events happened during my lifetime.

"For years I've watched black folks in this community bungle elections on positions far less significant than this one. We have decades of mudslinging and families falling out with each other, and I'm afraid that if we run one of the usual suspects in this election, those white folks will whip our asses like we stole the government mule.

"Chante, what you gotta ask yourself is if you believe that you'd give your best in representing the people of this district, that you'd be fair, that you'd be that leader we need around here. When my generation is dead and gone, who're we gonna leave things to? Your generation. I believe in you, and I'm willing to pump some scratch into your campaign and even serve on your kitchen cabinet. You'll need to pick a campaign manager and team, but I'll work with you behind the scenes. What's the worse thing that could happen? You'd be a well known lawyer, and that'd likely bring in more business for the firm, and you'll have established yourself as a mover-and-shaker, which is more valuable than you even realize."

Once Grady finished his somewhat over-the-top speech (comparing her to King and Obama?), Chante sat silently, letting his words sink in. She was still unsure that she would want to do this, but she didn't want to let Grady down. He seemed so passionate about her candidacy. Even she knew not to undervalue the currency of someone not only believing in you, but also putting his money where his mouth was.

"Can I sleep on it?" she finally said.

"Sure," Grady responded. "Give it some serious thought. And when you're ready, let's make some history."

## CHAPTER TWENTY-TWO

WHEN CHANTE HOUSE graduated from George Washington University Law School, she was the only person in her class to sit for the Mississippi bar. It wasn't that she was the only Mississippian in her class —there were definitely one or two others—but she was the only one who wanted to return to the state. When she mentioned this to her classmates, they openly questioned her as to why she would waste a degree from one of the best law schools in the country on a state that lazily ratified the 13th Amendment of the Constitution in 2013, a full one hundred and forty-eight years after it had become national law.

Even Chante's parents didn't see the point in returning to the Magnolia state, either, having spent the last ten years living abroad in Barbados. Being an only child, Chante was used to being alone, so it didn't bother her that she had to make her own decisions regarding her career. The only advice her parents offered was for her to do what made her happy, since they had already committed themselves to doing the same.

Chante figured that having a law degree from a top-tier law school would make getting a job in her home state a slam dunk. She'd originally had her eyes set on getting a job in the Jackson metro area doing either corporate law or litigation, representing companies with deep pockets. If she had gone to school ten years earlier, she would have probably pursued mass tort litigation, but when the state legislature decided to put an end to the massive punitive damages being leveled on defendant corporations back in 2003, the competition thinned out tremendously. By the time Chante graduated, it seemed as if most of the financial security she'd hoped for was tied up in doing defense or transactional work for corporations. And a GW pedigree was supposed to be the key to unlocking any door that stood in the way.

It didn't work out that way, though.

By the time she learned she had passed the bar exam, she still hadn't found a job and had taken to standing around at various county courthouses in the Jackson metro area, hoping to meet other lawyers who were hiring. She didn't know much about the actual practice of law, only what she had learned in law school, which amounted to studying how judges viewed cases—which was always subject to change.

That's when she stumbled upon Grady Sails. He had a short, round frame, his eyes appearing larger beneath the thick lenses of his glasses. He appeared to be in his seventies, and his white low-cut Afro was sprinkled with the occasional strand of dark brown hair. He looked distinguished and lively, but he also looked as though he were barely carving out a living. His clothing was rumpled and his brown cap-toed oxfords had a shiny, but worn-down, look. His crooked bow tie was orange and green, a monstrosity next to the charcoal grey blazer and navy blue slacks he was wearing. Yet beneath his fashion-challenged look was the glow of wisdom. It was that glow that caused Chante to approach him.

"Are you trying a case today?" she asked. She wanted to sound casual, as if she herself were in the Madison County courthouse that day doing the same thing.

"Not today. I'm just getting this order signed," he said, lifting up the file under his arm for emphasis. "Judge Pilar is slow as molasses, so I hope it don't take all damn day. I gotta two and half hour drive back to the office."

"Really?" Chante responded with interest. "Where do you practice?"

"Up in Daily. Round 'bout up near Columbus."

"Oh. I'm from Grenada."

"Grenada? You know the Waymon family?"

"Yeah, I know the Waymons. I went to school with Todd's son Freddy. Small world!"

The old man extended his hand. "I'm Grady Sails."

"I'm Chante House," she responded, shaking his hand.

"So where do you practice?" he asked.

Chante felt there was no point in being coy about wanting a job, so she blurted out, "I just passed the bar. I don't have a job yet. That's kind of why I'm here today."

Grady stared at her silently for a moment, his eyes looking gigantic behind his bifocals, and then let out a deep chuckle. "You came *here* to find a job? You might'a been better off goin' up near Oxford. These jokers 'round here are broke as a joke. Their money is funny, and their credit just ain't gon' get it."

Chante smiled. She liked him already. "At this point, I'm just looking for a job."

"Where did you go to law school?" he asked.

"George Washington."

"Shi-yat!" he said, as if he were cursing while doing a karate chop. "You'll have to pardon my language, but I thought you just said GW Law."

"I did."

"Shi-yat! Goddamn! How the hell did you find your way up in these sticks? You oughta be up in DC or New York or some place pulling down a grip of duckets."

His sense of humor caught her off guard and she found herself laughing heartily before responding. "I've always been a Southern girl, and I knew I wanted to come back here after law school. So here I am," she said, then added, "I've been interviewing around town. Most of the jobs were already sewn up before I sat for the bar and what's left out there seems to be going to grads of Ole Miss and Mississippi College."

Grady smiled. "Yeah, that alumni connection is really something, ain't it?"

Chante nodded.

"What is the world coming to when a beautiful woman can't get a job?"

Chante smiled. She hoped that the old man wasn't flirting. That would be the perfect end to a bad week if he were.

"Got plans for lunch?" he asked.

She pondered this for a second. If he *was* flirting, then he might take her acceptance as permission to move forward. But if he were actually going to offer her some guidance on her job search, she would be a fool to turn him down. She figured that it wouldn't hurt to get a free meal, and she could find out what his deal was then. If he turned out to be creepy, she'd leave him high and dry; if he turned out to have some gems of wisdom, it would have only cost her less than an hour of her time.

"I'm free."

"Well, let me see if I can find Judge Pilar and get this thing signed. I can meet you downstairs in the lobby."

"Sure," Chante said, watching the old man walk, or better yet, waddle, back into the courtroom, his legs stiff as his body swayed almost like a metronome. He really did look like Fred Sanford.

# CHAPTER TWENTY-THREE

OVER LUNCH, Grady asked Chante a series of questions: how were her grades in law school, what was her favorite course, did she write for any journals, did she participate in moot court competitions, and just about anything that would help to identify her knowledge of the law. Roughly halfway through answering these questions, Chante was convinced the old man had no romantic interest in her at all. If anything, the conversation seemed to suggest that he might be interviewing her for a job.

"Have you ever been to Daily before?" he asked between bites of his ham and cheese sandwich.

"I might've driven through there umpteen years ago, but I can't remember much about it."

Grady put his sandwich down. "It's a quiet little town, but it's a Mississippi town."

"What does that mean?"

"You're from Mississippi, right?"

"Yes."

"Then you ought to know what I mean."

Chante nodded, finally understanding. The race issue could never be ignored when one talked about

Mississippi, and by calling the town a Mississippi town, Grady was probably communicating that race was still very much a factor there. But that was nothing new for Chante. She could still hear her father say, "I prefer places in the South, because they let you know exactly where they stand, as opposed to trying to hide it like they do up North." But even Chante's father had apparently gotten sick of knowing where he stood and took his wife to a place where people of African descent were the clear majority.

"Think you might be interested in working there?"

"Why? Are you offering me a job?"

"Only if you're still looking for one."

Chante could feel her right leg wanting to bounce up and down with excitement, but she played it cool. "What kind of offer are you making?"

"Well, I have a small firm."

"How small?"

"Just me."

Chante almost laughed aloud, but caught herself. "What kind of law do you practice?"

"In Daily, all of us lawyers practice whatever comes through the front door. Mainly it's personal injury, social security disability, worker's compensation, medical malpractice, wills, deeds, and miscellaneous stuff."

It all sounded interesting, but Chante figured he could barely afford to pay himself, if his wardrobe was any indication of his income, and where would that leave her? "So what would my salary be?"

"Three thousand a month and a third of every case you close out after your salary and expenses are recouped."

"Well, okay then," Chante said. "I appreciate the offer, but I will need at least five thousand a month and half of whatever I settle beyond my salary, excluding expenses."

Grady smiled and stared at her for a moment. "You're negotiating with me. I like that. Is that the way they taught you up at GW?"

She couldn't tell whether he was insulting her or not. She had taken a negotiating course as a 2L and figured her counter-offer to be more than reasonable.

"Ever hear of the Boulwaristic style of negotiating?" Grady asked.

Chante tried to remember if she had, but nothing came to mind. "No, I don't think I have."

"Lemuel Boulware used to work for General Electric. He developed a way of negotiating where he would just put his best offer out there at the beginning, basically getting rid of the discussion and the back and forth. When it comes to my business, I'm all Boulwarism, all up and down through here. I only negotiate with defense attorneys and insurance companies, not employees. What I offered is the best I can do. If that's not good enough for you, I'm sorry to have wasted your time."

Chante swallowed hard, not knowing how to respond. Was he low-balling her to see what she would do, or was he telling the truth? She watched his eyes, nose, and lips, hoping for a tell-tell sign that he was bluffing, but his facial expression didn't change. She wished that there was someone she could talk to about his offer before responding to him, but there was no one. She had not talked to her parents much since they moved to Barbados, and she didn't want to burden them with this situation, because she already knew what her father and mother would say: "you're the one who will have to live with your decision either way it goes"—and that was not particularly helpful at this point.

Thirty-six thousand a year, plus bonuses, she pondered. That was nothing when compared to what her classmates were pulling down in various cities all along the East Coast. Many of them had healthy six figure offers before the third year of law school had even begun, yet here she was thinking about accepting a job that paid not even a third of the average starting salary for a George Washington Law School graduate. She started to tell him "no" on general principal. But this was the first offer she had gotten in the three months she had been looking for a job. Her savings were running low, and she could only continue staying in an extended stay for so long while she looked for a job.

Maybe she could accept the job and keep looking for another one in the meantime, she considered, or maybe just hold off on giving him an answer until she had exhausted whatever options there were that presented themselves to her during what was left of the week.

"Can I have a few days to think about it?" Chante asked.

Grady chuckled to himself. "I'm headed back to Daily when I leave here, and when I leave, so will my offer. Hey, look-a-here. I'm just trying to help you out. I've been getting along well for more than forty years. I just saw you and thought you could use a little help getting on your feet. If I could pay you more, I would, but you know how this economy is. But I tell you what. Maybe I can throw in some business cards and stationary, and who knows? If you stick around for a few years, maybe we could be partners."

"If I accept, then there will only be two lawyers in your firm. If I can bring in some clients, maybe we can talk about making me a partner sooner than later and we could split everything equally," Chante said, straining to propose a counteroffer.

"Let's just see how things work out. You learn to practice a little bit of law, and we can see where we stand in a year."

"Six months," Chante said.

Grady sighed, as he considered this. "We can evaluate in six months, but you would have to really be kicking up some sand for us to change the terms so soon. I'm open, though."

"So three grand a month, with a third of each case after I've recouped my salary, *and* I get an evaluation in six months to see if I can be made into a full partner?"

Grady nodded his head. "I can do that, but only if you give me your answer right now."

Chante lifted her hand slowly, trying to think of anything else she was missing. She stopped her hand in mid-air, just shy of his. "Benefits?"

"Hey, I'm a small practice. I'll be paying you as an independent contractor, so you'll have to figure that one out on your own."

Chante didn't like the idea of looking for her own healthcare plan at all and considered walking away from the table, but what would she be walking away to? Nothing, she knew.

"I know this is probably not what you had in mind when you passed the bar," Grady said, "but the truth is that I can probably teach you more about the practice of law than anyone else can at this point. Other lawyers will have you doing associate work, learning the ropes nice and slow. With me, I'll teach you all of the tricks of the trade that've allowed me to be in private practice this long. See, what some young lawyers think they can do is walk around with their textbooks from law school or their notes from the bar and charge people full price for their services. The truth is that age and treachery will trump youth and enthusiasm every single day of the week. I come from the kill or be killed generation of practicing law, so I'll make sure you can hold your own."

Chante listened to the old man, knowing that beggars couldn't be choosers. He was her only option at this point. He was the "bird in the hand." She knew she would accept his offer, but it was nothing to run home and brag about.

Grady Sails was just giving her an opportunity, nothing more, and when she thought about the money, her classmates, and her degree, she realized that an opportunity was really all she needed. If she was going to be as good as she thought she would be, then she would make much more than three thousand dollars a month.

She grasped his hand firmly. "I'm in."

# CHAPTER TWENTY-FOUR

THE FIRST THREE months of Chante's tenure at Sails and Associates went far better than she had expected. While the overall office space was relatively small, the practice stayed busy. She learned how to prepare deeds and wills, and she had already sent out some discovery documents on a few of the cases Grady had handed over to her to get her started. She felt like she was *really* practicing law, as opposed to hunkering down over a mountain of paperwork, billing hours deep into the night. She even had a few motions that were coming up on the docket over at the Humma County Courthouse. She would be presenting them in front of an actual judge!

The money was not as bad as she thought it would be. Although she still had yet to recoup her salary, she was making progress. In Daily, though, the cost of living was so low her thirty-six thousand dollars a year did not prevent her from having a decent lifestyle. Her apartment rent was only three hundred and fifty dollars a month, and that was for two bedrooms.

Socially, the town was a bit of a disappointment, she quickly learned. She was one of only a few black professionals in her age group, and from what she soon learned about the handful of available men in Daily, they were incredibly conceited and enjoyed going through women like toilet paper. The only thing that prevented Chante from completely throwing her hands in the air was that Daily was near a few other small towns. Maybe there were better options down the highway.

True to his word, Grady met with her weekly for an hour to share with her some of the "tricks of the trade." Already she had been able to prevent a summary judgment motion from killing one of her cases, thanks to the old man's advice.

Grady had told her it would be six months before he would review whether or not to promote her, and she figured that that was a fair amount of time, if she focused herself and did as much work as she could to learn as many different things as possible. Originally she thought she could accomplish that goal in less than six months, but she was sorely mistaken. Six months would be the absolute earliest she would even be in a position to request a promotion and say it with a straight face.

One thing she thought she was going to hate, but grew to appreciate, was that there were only three people at Sails and Associates, P.L.L.C.: Grady, Chante, and the secretary, Linda Swann, a forty-something black woman who wore large, circular glasses with eyewear cords hooked on either end. She looked like the black version of Dustin Hoffman's *Tootsie* character. She was nice and sweet, though, and while she did nothing to alleviate Chante's workload (Chante did all of her own drafting of documents and packaging of materials to mail out to other lawyers or insurance companies), Ms. Swann was a brilliant "people" person and was incredibly organized. Chante wondered how she had come to work there, but had never gotten around to asking Grady.

Maybe, when things took off (yes, she was becoming increasingly more positive about her future at Sails and Associates), they could bring in a paralegal and a case manager or two so that they could free up their time to take on more cases. Things were already starting to move at a pace Chante could barely keep up with.

But then Grady called her into his office one day and asked her to consider running for the senate seat in the newly gerrymandered district 44.

She had thought on it, and, in her mind, rejected the offer a thousands times, but now as she sat across from him two days later, she felt her body cramping with anxiety. What could she contribute as an elected official? It was not as easy a question to answer as she might have liked it to be. Of course, the salary, when paired with her current income, would be an improvement, but from her research, she would have to be away from the law office for at least three months out of the year, something Grady had already seemed to have understood, accepted, and encouraged.

"So did you get a chance to think about it?" Grady asked. "The clock is ticking. I need to know if you're in or out. Some of the usual suspects are already starting to beat their drums to gather support. None of them Negroes can win this thing, but it ain't never stopped them before."

Chante took a deep breath, hoping to calm her nerves. It didn't work. She had not felt this much pressure pricking her conscious since she learned that her parents were moving abroad, leaving her in this big country by herself. She eventually got used to the idea, as she knew she would get used to her decision here, but it didn't stop that initial gut-wrenching feeling that buzzed around her stomach, forcing her to shift uncomfortably in her seat.

"I'm gonna do it," she finally said. "I don't know the first thing about running for office, but I didn't know the first thing about practicing law either. The way I see it, I just have to learn by doing. It's been working well for me so far, so let's just hope things continue on that way."

Grady smiled so broadly that she could see the gold caps in the back of his mouth.

"Excellent!" he said, the whiskers around his mouth dancing up and down. "Well, the first thing you'll need to do is go down to the courthouse and declare yourself as a candidate."

When Chante left Grady's office, she thought her legs would feel lighter, but even in the walk over to the Humma County Courthouse, some four blocks away, her legs felt as if she were dragging bags of cement behind her.

## CHAPTER TWENTY-FIVE

CHANTE DIDN'T KNOW EXACTLY how Grady did it, but he managed to get all of the other potential senatorial candidates who were black to abstain from the election this time around, leaving just Chante and one other person, an older white lawyer named David McKlusky, whom she had heard was a millionaire.

While Grady refused to serve as Chante's campaign chair, he was working closely with her as a part of her kitchen cabinet, per his original promise. As a result, Chante had to find someone who could serve as her campaign manager, and after that, there would be several other positions that would need filling.

Having a limited circle of acquaintances, Chante went with whatever recommendations Grady offered. With his money, his advice, and his connections, she could not stop herself from wondering why it was not he who was running for this office instead of her. At times it seemed as if he were conducting some sort of crude experiment: take a virtually unknown person and have her run for an office at the top of the ticket. It was not like he had approached her to consider running for one of the county clerk positions (chancery or circuit) or even the county prosecuting attorney position; he had catapulted her up the ladder to an office that would not only be on the ballot for Humma County, but the ballots for Boxun County and Mudbone County as well. Rather than feel like she was trying to fill shoes entirely too big for the experience she was bringing to the table (college, law school, and now her first real job, all at the age of twenty-five), she worried primarily about letting down this man who had put so much trust, energy, and money into her candidacy. She knew that she would be the one to govern, not he, but she simply couldn't fathom his motivation for doing any of this. After all, he had hired her and was now propping her up politically. Everything that had happened to her this far exceeded what one would associate with even an altruistic person.

The campaign chair that Chante selected (and whom Grady had recommended) was a political science professor named Toni Savage from the local state university. The way that Grady proposed Toni to Chante was riddled with even greater contradictions, though.

"She is by far the most talented political thinker in our county, although she keeps a very low public profile. So while she's sharper than a shark's tooth, she's got the people skills of Howard Hughes. Oh, yeah, and she's a dyke, too."

"I believe the politically correct term is 'lesbian,'" Chante offered.

"Hell, give me some credit for not calling her a bull dagger. Shi-yat."

"So she's gay. So what? Is that why she's a recluse?"

"Chante, this here is Mississippi, where they still fly that rebel flag high and mighty like the South didn't get their asses handed to them in the Civil War. These people are about as conservative as you can get—even the black folks. Most people around here respect her, but every woman thinks Toni wants her, and every man is afraid that Toni will turn out his woman, so I guess if I were her, I probably wouldn't fuck with these country bumpkins too much either. Still, she knows her stuff, and I'd bet on my wife's sweet soul, may she rest in peace, that Toni Savage is the only person who could run your campaign the right way, official, with none of that nigger shit that saddles the other candidates out there chasing their tails for the other offices."

Chante immediately set up a meeting with Toni Savage and invited her to come by the Sails and Associates office.

The first thing that Chante noticed about Toni was that she was neatly dressed, her pant suit impeccable. Toni's hair was trimmed low and carefully maintained with easy, natural waves. Her face was round and pretty, but beneath her suit, she looked not only large, but solid, as well.

"It's good to meet you, Professor Savage," Chante said.

"The pleasure is mine," Toni responded, shaking Chante's hand.

Chante escorted her to the conference room and immediately launched into why she had contacted the political science professor.

"I'm new to this community, but I feel that I have some great ideas for the people in District 44, and you come highly recommended."

Toni smiled, absorbing the compliment. "Well, I appreciate it. Grady and I go way back. I used to serve as an expert witness for a few of his cases. But before we get started, I have to ask you one question. Was it your idea to run for this seat or Grady's? Be honest."

Chante chuckled. "I guess you already know the answer to that question."

Toni nodded. "He must really think a lot of you."

"Yeah. I guess. It all seems like a bit much, though," Chante said. "I mean, he should probably be the one running for office, given that he knows a lot more about all of this stuff than I do."

Toni lifted an eyebrow, measuring Chante's demeanor. "You don't know, do you?"

"Know what?"

Toni leaned in closer to Chante. In a slow and deliberate voice she said, "He's not doing well."

"What do you mean not doing well? Like sick?"

"He hasn't talked to you about his health in all the time you've been here?"

"No," Chante responded, trying desperately to steel her mind. "You have to tell me what's going on. I just moved all of my stuff here to Daily for this man. I'm starting to freak out."

Toni sighed. "He finished a round of radiation a while back and swore he was done with it. In fact, I thought he would have closed down this practice. But then I heard about you coming to work here."

Chante's stomach burned with the hot pain of fear. She couldn't feel her limbs, the shock overwhelming her. "Why?" was all she could manage.

"My guess is that he saw something in you that made him want to help you and figured that he'd have enough time to teach you everything you needed to know to be successful here in Daily."

Chante swallowed, but her throat felt as if a large ball of peanut butter were stuck there and wouldn't go down. She had not known Grady all that long, but he was now her closest confidante and the person responsible for helping her maintain her sanity in her new vocation.

Toni sat patiently for a moment, allowing this new information to sink in, but when Chante made no effort to open her mouth again, Toni reached in her pocket and pulled out a business card, handing it to Chante. "I know you have a lot on your mind right now, so I'm going to just leave this here with you. If you want me to help out with your campaign, I'd be happy to. But right now I'm going to give you a little time to yourself. If you need anything in the meantime, just give me a call."

Chante nodded and then rose to shake Toni's hand. "Thank you," she said, her voice still weak, her mind restless with questions.

## CHAPTER TWENTY-SIX

"WHY DIDN'T YOU TELL ME?" Chante asked Grady the following morning, shortly after he arrived at the office.

"I take it Toni must've told you about the cancer."

"Uh, *yes*," Chante said sarcastically. "Were you ever going to tell me?"

"Sure. In my own time."

"Grady, I moved all the way to Daily to practice law with you. I'm busting my ass day in and day out to become your partner so that we can do this together. *Together!*"

Grady lifted his hands. "Hold on. Let's calm down for a minute. I'll explain everything to you. Just give me a minute."

Chante closed her eyes and took a deep breath before opening them. "Talk."

"Okay," Grady said. "A few years back, a little while after my wife passed on, I went in for a checkup and the doctor told me I had prostate cancer. I got it removed, and for a while everything was okay. Then it started coming back. I did the chemo and the radiation off and on, and I had just stopped my treatments about a month before I met you."

Chante's eyes brightened. "So it's not too late for you to start back up then."

Grady shook his head. "Chante, I'm an old man. I'm eight-two. I've had a good life. Plus, I miss my Darlene. I figure whatever days I have left are the ones the good Lord'll give me."

"And how much time is that? I know the doctors gave you an estimate."

"Maybe a year."

"A year!" Chante was livid. Suddenly the election seemed incredibly insignificant.

"I know I can do more than a year, though. I have some serious will power. See, Chante, you're giving me hope, and that's something the doctors can't give me right now. I want to see the best for you. I want to see you achieve your goals. I want everything for you that I couldn't have for myself, and I'm prepared to help you see it through."

Chante tried to hold in her tears but couldn't. They streamed onto her cheeks openly, and she didn't care to wipe them away. "I just don't understand. You're doing all of this for me. Why? Why do I deserve your generosity?"

Grady shrugged his shoulders. "I don't know. I guess it just feels right. Maybe you'll help me to get into heaven," he joked.

"That's not funny," she responded. "What am I supposed to do when you're gone?"

"Well, I'm gonna teach you how to run this office while you learn the law. I'll also add your name to the checking accounts. And if things go well with this election, you'll either be a state senator or a well-known attorney with a growing client base. That should give you everything you need to make your mark here. And oh, yeah," he added, "I'll be making you a partner."

Chante had thought she would be excited when she heard those words. She had imagined that she would walk into Grady's office at the end of six months and get the news and they would go out to dinner to celebrate. She had only been at the firm for four months and the way she was receiving the news of her partnership was so anticlimactic that she felt overcome with melancholy instead of joy.

"I need some time to process all of this," she said.

Grady nodded. "Take off the rest of the afternoon, and we can talk tomorrow."

She stood up slowly. Her plan was to exit the room quickly, but when Grady rose from his desk, a gentlemanly gesture, she walked over to him and embraced him deeply, as if he were one of her own relatives. He squeezed her in his warm arms, and she almost cried on his shoulder but held herself together just long enough to get back to her office and collapse in tears at her desk.

# CHAPTER TWENTY-SEVEN

AS THE WEEK DRAGGED ON, two things became increasingly clearer: (1) it was going to take Chante a while to get over the bomb that Grady dropped on her, and (2) selecting Toni as her campaign manager was turning out to be a stroke of genius. Not only was Toni giving her a good crash course in local politics, she was also proving to be a good person to confide in, in general. Chante had no doubt that, in a town where she still knew very few people, Toni would easily become a true friend, someone who would keep Daily, Mississippi, from being as socially boring as it had been initially.

Toni was also a great comfort in helping Chante cope with all of the bad news that Grady had laid upon her. Things were still difficult to absorb, but it helped to have someone—other than Grady—to talk to about these things. She still didn't know what would happen should she lose the election and Grady pass away. Could she really stay in Daily and forge ahead, or would she need to explore other options, namely leaving the area to try to do something different with her life? Her parents had invited her to come spend some time in Barbados with them, and while she liked the idea of a long hiatus in the Caribbean, she relished the idea of remaining in the United States of America, pursuing her particular vision of the American dream. Still, given the volatility of her mood, she refused to rule out anything at this particular point in time.

"One thing that you have working in your favor is that a lot of the people around here know that District 44 was designed to produce a black senator," Toni said one evening while sitting across from Chante at her dining room table.

"Well, I guess that does work in our favor."

"In theory it should, but the thing is that there're also a lot of other people out there who might not know that or particularly care about it. You have to always count on most of your constituents knowing far less than you would want them to know about any particular issue—even after you've been elected. With the Internet, there's so much inaccurate information being spread far too quickly for anyone to really control it. That's the reason why you have to be as clear as possible on your platform. If a person can misunderstand you or misconstrue your words, then it is likely that they will. And there is a lot at stake in this election so you should hope for the best but prepare for the worst."

Chante nodded. "I keep asking myself if I'm in over my head, like I might have really taken a big bite off of something that I don't have even the slightest chance of being able to digest."

Toni chuckled. "I'm sure all politicians feel that way at some point during a campaign. And it's okay for you to feel that way. You just can't wear those emotions on your sleeve when you leave your house. You can't show insecurity and doubt when you're campaigning, and to be honest, you're always campaigning. When you go to the grocery store, you're campaigning. If you're out getting your mail and you see someone, you're campaigning. And when I say 'campaigning,' I mean that you're smiling and offering warm and reassuring conversation to people."

Chante nodded. She looked down at the massive binder Toni had put together for her that contained all of the numbers from previous county elections for the past decade, along with the most recent voter rolls saved on thumb drives that were placed inside the inner pockets of the six-inch binder. Chante was overwhelmed by how full it was. How much time had Toni put into creating this thing? At that moment Chante was glad that Toni was volunteering, because she had no idea of how much something like this would cost if she were charged for this mountain of data.

"So," Chante said, "can you tell me about David McKlusky? I've only seen him in passing and we have yet to go head-to-head in the courtroom."

Toni interlocked her fingers and sat back in her chair. "I moved here about ten years ago, and he'd been in Daily for a while before I got here. His reputation is okay. He tends to represent businesses, and everyone knows that he and his family have money. In fact, I think that his wife is related to Billy Stamps, who, last time I heard, was worth around two hundred million or so."

"Good lord!" Chante said, unable to fathom anyone in the state of Mississippi with that kind of money. She had heard of mass tort lawyers who earned ridiculous amounts of money at the close of the 20th century, but having a net worth in the nine figure range was obscene!

"And you can definitely count on him outspending

you in this election, so don't even feel like that's a pissing contest you want to enter."

"But I thought that the axiom normally went like this: he who spends the most money wins the election," Chante said.

"That's usually the case in most races. Of course, President Obama proved that one wrong, though. Governor Romney outspent him but still lost. That just illustrates that there're a number of other factors that go into winning an election. And we're going to use everything that we have at our disposal to try to even the odds for you."

Chante sighed. She had always known that she would be the David to McKlusky's Goliath, but she didn't know what would constitute the sling that she would need to overcome her mountain of an opponent. "So what were you thinking we should do?"

"Well," Toni started, "we need to make sure that black people, particularly the young people, get out and vote for you. If that group remains apathetic to this type of election, then McKlusky will win. The demographics of Humma, Boxun, and Mudbone are clearly in your favor—that is if people actually go to the polls. So the key is to get them fired up for you. We'll use social media, like Facebook, Twitter, and Instagram, and we'll enlist other young people of influence to get out the word for you. As you can imagine, though, you'll need to have more of the hustlers and hood-savvy guys in your corner since the number of professional blacks is too small and lacks sufficient influence to get the turnout that you'll need."

Chante nodded, trying to absorb everything. "So do you know any of these people you're referring to? Because I don't."

"If I don't, then I know someone who does. Plus,

I'm going to offer extra credit to my political science students to come over here to Daily and help out with the campaign. Many of them are good at doing the type of street team marketing that you're going to need. Plus, young people respond better to other young people."

"Thank you. That would be great!"

"No problem. But what I'll need for you to do is to think about your platform and where you stand on issues like education, crime, and the economy. The primary will essentially be the general election because there's no Republican candidate, so you'll need to play a moderate role going forward, no matter how liberal or conservative you might actually be. You're in Mississippi, as you already know, and people here can be flexible, but it sometimes takes a little time, so you have to play to the center. It's like this: you can pull the teeth of tiger, but you might want to do it when he is asleep as opposed to awake."

Chante laughed uncomfortably. Toni was essentially telling her what her positions should be on the topics she mentioned. Did what Chante actually think of these things even matter at the end of the day? Maybe. Probably not.

"So what do we do next?" Chante asked.

"We get your website and social media accounts going and start making contact with the movers and shakers in the various precincts throughout the three counties. You need to meet as many people as you possibly can if you want to beat a man who's been a part of this community for nearly two decades. That's how Bill Clinton ended up with the Democratic nomination in 1992. More people had met him in person than they had other candidates, so they voted for him. Don't ever feel like you're above asking any single person for his or her vote. We need every single vote we can get to win this election."

"Do you really believe I can win?"

Chante expected to hear Toni wax poetic with some anecdote where a novice, one that was politically inexperienced, had won an election when all of the odds were stacked against her, but she didn't. Instead, she responded simply, "Yes."

And that was good enough for Chante.

## CHAPTER TWENTY-EIGHT

CHANTE SOON DISCOVERED that she was better at meeting new people than she thought she'd be. As an only child, she had always been quiet and to herself growing up, so she viewed her natural disposition to be that of an introvert. When Toni mentioned she would need to go around "glad-handing" voters, the idea made her terribly nervous. She was not one given to small talk, and she feared that she would overcompensate for her inability to talk about casual things by going into academic arguments about how she would make an excellent senator for District 44. Much to her relief, though, she discovered that the best way to engage people you didn't know was to smile, be polite, and listen to their concerns.

When she first arrived in Daily, Grady had sat her down during one of their weekly meetings and explained that listening was the key to being a successful lawyer.

"Chante, one of the biggest places where young lawyers make mistakes with their clients is that they don't listen to a goddamn person the first. A lot of them are feeling so high and mighty because they passed the bar exam that they like to hear themselves talk up a damn storm. That could be the kiss of death on which cases to take and which ones to let go on their merry way," Grady had said. "See, a lot of times clients will tell you what *they* think is important, and often times what they think is important is different than what you may come to realize is *actually* important. If you're a lawyer going down a checklist, you might miss something big. I remember this one time I had a case that I thought was a slam dunk until I found out that the person in the room with me wasn't even the person who could have signed me up as the lawyer for the case. No fucking authority whatsoever. Just a nosy ass relative trying to get some information so they could be the smart one in the family to tell everybody else what to do. Another time I thought I had a Moby Dick and found out that my client had so much contributory negligence that it made taking on the case unnecessary, especially since I was doing it all on contingency. If I had been billing his ass by the hour, none of that would have mattered, but that would have been too much like right."

Chante absorbed all of this. Grady's point was that in addition to asking all of the right questions, you had to follow the potential client on tangents from time to time to find out what was really going on. It was like a question on the bar exam, when you thought about it: you read the first part of the question thinking that it was a question about one type of law, but by the time you got to the final prompt, you realized it was actually about an entirely different set of laws altogether.

The bottom line, underscored repeatedly by both Grady Sails and Toni Savage, was to simply listen. At worst, someone gave you some information that was harmless and irrelevant; at best, they gave you something invaluable that you would not have otherwise gotten.

So as Chante began taking her newly minted street team door-to-door, she realized that people were responding favorably to her. Even some of the young men she met flattered her endlessly, begging for the chance to date her, which was a bit ironic, because when she was looking for someone to go out with, there was no one around. Toni encouraged her to milk her looks for everything she could get. "Kennedy," she would say, "won a lot of women's votes because he had the good sense to present himself well on television. Many people respond to attractive candidates."

Even a number of the ministers throughout various communities expressed an interest in supporting her, which was a good thing since she had learned that they still held a great deal of influence over their congregations when it came to elections.

She was getting such a favorable response from the potential voters she encountered that she allowed herself to fantasize a little bit about a victory. Her mood had also improved a great deal, which allowed her to be more open with Grady about his plans for the law practice.

During the time that she had been upset with him, things had felt very *off* in her life. Now everything was hitting on all cylinders: she and Grady were not only on good terms, but furthering the deep bond that they had previously begun to develop, and Toni was working miracles for her, turning a no-name candidate into a frontrunner for state senator.

While out knocking on doors in the county one Saturday afternoon, her cell phone rang. It was Grady.

"Hey!" Chante said, stepping away from the house she had just finished leaving a flyer for.

"Chante, I need you to drop by the office later this afternoon. Just you, okay?" Grady said.

"Why? What's wrong?"

"Nothing's *exactly* wrong, but I need to discuss something with you as soon as you have a free minute."

Chante didn't know why, but she felt her stomach tremble with worry. There was just something disquieting about the tone of Grady's voice. "I can come straight to the office now, if you need me to."

"I'm actually over at Miss Helen's getting a bite to eat, but I can meet you over there in half an hour."

"Okay," Chante said.

When she hung up the phone, she knew, without a doubt, whatever Grady had to tell her would probably bring her spirits down from the elevated high she was riding.

She just hoped it was not something about his health. While she was still adjusting to his news, she had hardly braced herself for what they both knew would be the inevitable.

She said a silent prayer for Grady, went back to her car, and headed on over to the office to work on a few cases while she waited for him.

## CHAPTER TWENTY-NINE

GRADY SAT at the head of the conference table, his face a little ashen, but he did not otherwise show any signs of discomfort. "I was sitting in Miss Helen's restaurant when I overheard some people talking about your campaign."

"Yeah. What about it?" asked Chante.

"This is all my fault, because I knew something like this could've happened. But you know how you think that people grow up and get smarter? Well, that's not always the case."

Chante shrugged. "Grady, what are you talking about?"

"I recommended Toni Savage to you because, by all accounts, she is one of—if not *the* best—political thinker in this county."

"I'm glad that you did. She's been wonderful! I really feel like I'm getting the hang of this thing. I believe we have a great shot at winning the election."

Grady lowered his head. "In an ideal world you would win this election, hands down. But there're a few things you should probably know about."

Chante was starting to get aggravated with his

beating around the bush and wanted to blurt out, "Just tell me!" but she trusted his rationale for parsing out the information. Apparently she needed to brace herself for what was to come.

"Word is starting to get around that you and Toni have a *thing* going on," Grady said.

"A thing? You mean like we're romantically involved?"

Grady nodded.

'Well, we don't."

"Yeah, I know this, but these ignorant backwater folks don't."

"So what does it mean if they think that about me anyway?"

"In a small town like Daily, more than you'd like to believe."

Chante shook her head as if waving off the nagging buzzing of a bee. "I've been working with you all this time, and I've never heard anyone accuse you and me of having a relationship with each other."

"Well, most of the folks around here know that I had prostate cancer. Even folks who spend all day watching daytime TV and gossiping about their neighbors know that getting your whole prostate removed can really mess with your love life."

"Can't we just ignore the rumors and keep campaigning hard? I mean, why should we dignify ignorant assumptions?"

"Well, Toni is definitely an out lesbian, and the fact that the two of you spend so much time together, people are going to continue to think the worst."

Chante was livid. "How is being a lesbian a bad thing? These people have never heard of the 14th Amendment or the civil rights movement?"

"To folks around here, the civil rights movement was about rights for black people, not all people."

Chante was not particularly bothered that people had misconstrued her sexuality. The right guy would put an end to that mess anyway, but she felt personally offended that Toni was being attacked for something that was hardly worth batting an eye at in Washington, DC, where she'd spent the past three years. Would people really not vote for her for associating with a gay woman? Or even being perceived as gay? Were people really that silly? And if they were, did she really want to be the person representing them in the state legislature? She knew on issues of civil rights she would always vote liberally, so were her personal convictions truly at odds with the people she was asking to vote for her? She hoped like hell that they were not, but what Grady was telling her was not bringing her a great deal of comfort.

"So what should I do?" she finally asked.

"Clearly, the ultimate decision is up to you, but if you wanted to push back in a passive aggressive way, you should start dating."

The idea of dating someone just to prove her sexuality was offensive in too many ways to even begin to enumerate. Considering the women who had struggled for equal rights throughout the history of the country, not to mention those black women who shouldered the burden of two levels of oppression, Chante's being forced—or better, coerced—into behaving in a manner to make herself more palatable to the masses would be a slap in the face of progress. Would she be selling herself out to go out on a few dates?

Probably so.

But what if she met the right person and went out on a date. That would be normal, right? Granted, this looming situation wouldn't make it feel as normal as it should, though.

"Do you have any suggestions on guys I could go out with?" Chante asked, and deep inside of her she could feel a piece of her heart whisper, "Ca-ching!" as if she were beginning the slow process of selling out.

## CHAPTER THIRTY

THE LAST RELATIONSHIP Chante had been in was during her second year of law school, when she had made the egregious mistake of dating another law school student, Kofi Banks. At first the relationship started with them studying together for their shared Corporate Law course. From studying together, they evolved their relationship into getting drinks on Friday nights. Then came the Saturday afternoon movie matinees. When he invited her to church one Sunday, she realized that the relationship might have been evolving into more than just a platonic friendship. After all, there is a big difference between getting a few drinks at a bar in Adams Morgan and getting dressed to accompany someone to worship at their home church.

Armed with the idea that what they had was special, she allowed him to begin spending the night at her house. He was smart, handsome, and a great student with job prospects already lined up. Even more, she had found one of the few African-American men at the law school who was even showing her the slightest bit of interest. (Many of the other brothers were dating all nationalities, and she herself had been on a few dates with guys who were not African American, although nothing lasted for more than a few dates.)

Kofi had been her first boyfriend since she graduated from Hampton University, and she figured that the next step for the two of them was engagement and then marriage. After all, what else were grown people who were compatible and in love supposed to do?

Kofi, however, dropped the ball when the spring semester ended, shortly before he was to start his summer internship with a corporate law firm in Boston.

"I just don't know if I'm ready to be in a relationship this serious," he said. "I'm still trying to get my life together. I have no idea of where I'll be working after graduation, and I think it would be unfair to have you waiting for me while I figured these things out."

Yes, it had been classic male bullshit, as if he were reading verbatim from the *Sorry Ass Guy's Handbook*.

It all hurt much more than she cared to admit. Somehow her identity had become entwined with his, and she had spent hours upon hours daydreaming about their future lives together: what cars they would drive, where they would live, how many kids they would have, where they would vacation, and even what charities they would volunteer their time and money with. In retrospect, she realized she had gone a bit overboard with a lot of things in the relationship, but she had not told him even half of what she'd been fantasizing about. The small bit that she had shared (and that he had contributed his own ideas toward as well) had apparently spooked him, in spite of the way he pretended to act around her.

For a while she wondered if she could do better than Kofi Banks. There were some guys who had a few of Kofi's qualities, but they didn't have them all. Even more, when Kofi was with her (and into her), he had all of the qualities that she had ever wanted from a man—and had those very qualities in spades. When he left her, she was forced to think that maybe there was something in her that was not all that it could have been. Was she not good enough for her ideal man? That was the question she would force upon herself and wrestle with unnecessarily until she graduated and the bar exam became a more pressing matter.

Now, she considered herself married to the law, an arrangement that she knew would only last so long before she built up the nerve to stick her toe back into the dating waters again. She just had to get over her fear of having her heart broken, if that were even possible. But from what Grady was telling her, she had to get off her behind and stop being afraid. Her political future, it seemed, depended on her just making herself appear more like the heterosexual woman she actually was.

The idea still irritated her for a variety of reasons, the main one being that she shouldn't have had to perform her personal life for public consumption. The other thing that bothered her was the homophobia at the heart of people's accusations.

Grady had, however, arranged a blind date with a young attorney from nearby Columbus. He had driven to pick her up in his dark BMW sedan, a vehicle clearly designed to alert his clients that he was a "winner" (and would help them to win, too!). His name was Winston Roosevelt, III. Even his name smacked of the kind of success that every young corporate lawyer wanted upon graduation from law school—before real life set in and forced one to reevaluate his or her priorities. In many ways, Winston reminded her of Kofi, which was not a good thing. Still, she decided to reserve judgment and go on the date, if only to show her appreciation to Grady for the trouble he had gone through to set it up. (She told Toni about her up-coming "date," but did not bother with its curious timing because she didn't want Toni to feel offended or to judge her for her decision.)

The unspoken understanding between Chante and Winston was that the date had to take place in Daily, as opposed to Columbus. It, sadly, was important that people see them together. Even more, the right people had to see them. As a result, they had dinner at the local soul food restaurant owned by Miss Helen, the same one in which Grady had overheard the gossiping. Even the time of the date coincided with a time in which the largest number of people would be present. It was the first time Chante had ever felt that one of her dates had been "produced," much in the way a movie would have been.

She was also dressed to impress, in what her friends from Hampton University would have called "business hoochie" attire, a black dress that, while designed to be formal, if worn one size smaller, made even a monk sworn to celibacy take a second look. As she sashayed in front of Winston Roosevelt, III, she knew she had his full attention. He would ask for a second and third date and possibly much more. That was not even a concern of Chante's. But she knew while she might have dressed in a sexy way, she was not an *easy* person, so Winston would be window shopping for quite a while, if he was even around long enough to do that.

The other men in the restaurant were unable to avoid looking at her, which made her little plan even that much more effective. She looked stunning, and there was a man on her arm. What this seemed to say to most men was that, if they stepped up their games, they too, might have a shot at a woman like her. Oh, the vanity of it all made her head hurt. She knew if she made it through the night, the next date would be much more low key.

"So how have you enjoyed being back in Mississippi?" Winston asked, after learning that she had grown up in Grenada.

"It's been nice so far. This election has taken up a lot of my time, though."

"I can only imagine," Winston said, smiling. Clearly, he knew he was handsome, Chante mused.

"The good thing is that we only have a few more weeks until the primary."

"Can I ask you a question?" Winston ventured.

"Sure. And you don't have to ask me if you can ask a question. Feel free to just ask it."

He smiled again, and this time she noticed that he had a dimple on his left cheek. "Okay. Well, what made you want to run for office so soon after returning to the area?"

It was a fair question. "Some times opportunities present themselves and you don't have much of a choice but to act. Remember when Obama decided to run for president in 2007? Or when Martin Luther King, Jr. took the reigns of the Montgomery Bus Boycott at the age of twenty-six? Sometimes coming from outside of the establishment is a good thing," Chante responded, feeling like a big sap for regurgitating one of Grady's earlier arguments in favor of her candidacy.

"Wow," Winston said flatly. "I can tell that you're really something. Few people would compare themselves to Obama or King."

"No. That's not what I meant," she responded quickly.

"I'm just messing with you," he said, smiling again.

As dinner progressed she was surprised at how little he talked about himself and how much interest he showed in what she thought about things. She had not expected that of him. She had taken him for a man who was a bit more self-absorbed. If he was in fact that man, he was doing an amazing job of concealing it.

After dinner, they went for a walk through the well-lit portion of the city park, stopping at a large gazebo to talk. Winston remained the quintessential gentleman, and while he appeared to be interested, he was far more patient than she had anticipated. He touched her only when assisting her to the car, to the table, up the stairs of the gazebo, and eventually down the stairs and back to her car. Never did he once touch her just for the sake of touching her.

Then the idea hit her. The irony of it was so explosive that she almost burst out laughing when the date was over. Was Winston Roosevelt, III gay? Wouldn't that be a hilarious turn of events? Had she spent the night being a beard for a guy who was doing her a somewhat similar favor? If he was, she couldn't really be mad at either him or Grady.

It didn't matter anyway. She'd had a great time, and she was not looking for anything romantic anyway. She definitely had the patience to find out what the situation was with him when she had more time and energy to commit to the process.

## CHAPTER THIRTY-ONE

AFTER SEVERAL MORE "DATES" with Winston, activities that Toni quickly ascertained were designed to combat the rumors she herself had heard a while back, Chante was finally beginning to rebound in the court of public opinion, as far as she was able to tell. Up until that moment, Chante had been running her race without any real concern for what David McKlusky's camp was doing. Both candidates had surprisingly made it to within a few weeks of the election without ever slinging any mud or insults at the other. This was not something that escaped Grady's attention.

"The way you guys are running against each other, you might as well kiss and take each other out for a drink after the votes are tallied," he said.

Chante laughed. "I've seen enough negative campaign ads on TV, the radio, and the Internet to last a lifetime."

"Spoken like someone in her twenties," Grady said, stifling his own laughter.

"I want people to vote for me, not against him."

"Well, whether they vote for you or against him, they're still votes that count in your favor. It's nice to be above the fray, but keep in mind that the only thing that matters is the final tally of the votes."

Chante understood this all too clearly. She had continued canvassing Humma County and had hit every neighborhood in all of the precincts that were a part of her district there. She had also made a few trips over to Boxun County and Mudbone County. While she hadn't met every single person on her visits, she had met far more people than she expected. Most of them had been friendly toward her, but she sensed that some of them, particularly younger black women, seemed to be unimpressed with her. A few of them seemed as if they really despised her, but how could you despise someone you had never met before? After a little thought, she realized that this was the backlash from her dates with Winston. Maybe her flaunting of herself in public, albeit more tastefully than other women might have done under similar circumstances, had angered them. She didn't know if it was jealousy or something else, but if she were a woman who over-heard her man talking to his boys about another woman, she would have probably been a little less inviting herself. Maybe it was another vain thought, Chante considered, but she was a black woman and sensed that she knew the behavior of other black women when they felt threatened by something.

"I want you to see something," Grady said, pulling Chante from her thoughts. He handed her the Professional Limited Liability Company Operating Agreement for Sails and Associates, along with the necessary paperwork to make her a partner in the practice, and a form for a name change for the company. "We'll also need to go over to the bank tomorrow so I can add your name to the accounts."

As Chante combed through the materials, the magnitude of everything hit her. Grady was really going through with all of this.

"The only thing I ask is that you take care of Ms. Swann after I am gone. She's been here with me at the firm for over twenty years, through thick and thin, and as long as you have this practice, I would like for you to keep a job for her here. You would be surprised at how many times she's saved my ass over the years. And just as an overall rule of thumb, if you ever have to pay someone, make sure you're paying someone who is representing the face of your business to the outside world. Ms. Swann is old school, with impeccable manners. The more professional you look to the public, the better your practice will run. People out there don't need to see how we sweat our asses off back here at our desks, negotiating on their behalf and trying to salvage cases that we should have never signed up in the first place. And to be honest, they shouldn't ever have to know that stuff, the same way a child shouldn't have to know about the sacrifices a parent makes."

Chante nodded. "I understand. I would never think of letting Ms. Swann go."

"That's good to hear." Grady paused for a moment. "I will do everything in my power to help you win that senate seat."

"I know."

"I'm serious. There's no way I am going to let David McKlusky win, if I can help it. Not again."

"Again? What do you mean?" Chante asked.

"I had a case against him about fifteen years ago, *Ledbetter v. Stamps Plastic Works Corp.* The dirty, underhanded shit that guy pulled off caused us to lose the case. My clients had developed respiratory diseases—and eventually cancer—in behind some of the chemicals they had been using in certain parts of their

Jackson factory. David and those other jokers dumped mountains of useless shit on me at the end of the discovery period, deposed my clients for three days to the point of mental fatigue, pulled expert witnesses out of their asses and dumped them on the pretrial order at the last minute, leaving me no time to depose them. I lost my damn shirt on that case," Grady said.

"So this is personal?"

Grady sighed. "Chante, politics is always personal."

"So you *used* me?" The thought paralyzed Chante with fear.

"I'm not using you to get even with him. No. I wouldn't do that. And I'm a halfway decent Christian aiming to get into heaven soon, so no, I wouldn't use you to get even with him. I would, however, do whatever I could to make sure the people of this county were left in the hands of a person with character and positive motives. That's not David McKlusky. Chante, that's you. You're the person who is going to save this town, this county, this district from that man."

Chante blinked her eyes rapidly, trying to absorb Grady's words. She was still confused.

"Chante, you're the good guy in this battle, better than I could have ever been. You might not see that now, but trust me, you are the one who is going to save us from ourselves."

"Who is the 'us' here?"

"The people who have fought the fight so long that we can't see beyond our fists. You are better than that."

Chante sat quietly, her brain teetering between being upset about being misled and feeling the need to become Grady's champion.

"So this paperwork," Grady started, placing his hand on the pages in front of him, "will make your partnership official."

Chante lifted her pen from the table and placed her palm down on the last page. "I hope you're right about all of this," she said, allowing the nib of the pen to brush the paper.

She waited for Grady to respond, but he only watched the movement of her hand as it finished her signature and lifted from the page.

## CHAPTER THIRTY-TWO

"CHANTE, ARE YOU AWAKE?" Toni asked, her voice sharp and urgent.

"*Now* I am."

Chante sat up in her bed and looked at the digital clock on the night stand. It was 6:00 a.m. Dread filled her so quickly that she almost started to cry. For Toni to call at this time of the morning must have meant bad news, and the only bad news she could think of was that something had happened to Grady.

"You might have just won this election," Toni said.

"What do you mean?"

"Your only opponent is about to be arrested for murder."

Chante swept her legs over the edge of the bed and shook her head to wake herself up completely. "What?"

"Okay. I have a friend who works over at the police department, and the word is that David McKlusky's daughter called to tip the police off that her father had gotten drunk and started rambling about killing her ex-boyfriend. Well, they found the boy earlier this morning. He had been hit by a car and left on the side of the road."

None of this made any sense to Chante, and she didn't know what to say. It all sounded like some crazy made-for-TV movie that would only be shown during the wee hours of the morning.

"Why would he kill his daughter's ex-boyfriend?" Chante asked, although she had a number of other questions that were bubbling around her head as well.

"You sitting down?"

"Yeah."

"His daughter was dating a black kid who apparently was passing for white."

Chante shook her head, confused and upset. What the hell kind of town was she living in where a prominent member of the community could commit a hate crime while he was running for public office? And in the twenty-first century, too? The thought alone was scary and reminded her of the reason she had left Mississippi originally to go to college and law school in larger cities farther north along the eastern seaboard.

"I can't believe this," she said, leaning forward and placing her elbows on her knees.

"I know. The funny thing is that no one really knew the kid was black except for a few people. Apparently, his daughter was already transferring to Adams Academy, that white school across town, to put some distance between her and the boy," Toni said, before adding, "It's funny how things come together in Humma County."

Chante didn't know what to think of any of this, but her heart went out to the boy's parents. The whole idea of something like that happening in a community where death among young people was rare simply reinforced just how little had changed since the days when black people were lynched at will. Apparently, Mississippi would forever be scarred by its treatment of black people.

"So what do we need to do? Issue a statement of condolence? I don't know how this works, Toni."

"In a town this small, there's no need to issue any kind of statement. You will need to publicly show support for the family, though. Depending on what his family decides to do about the funeral, you might want to offer your condolences in whatever manner is the most tasteful."

"What was his name?" Chante asked.

"Brent Edwards."

"Lord, what is the world coming to?"

"You want to hear something even stranger?" Toni asked.

"What?"

"About a year ago another black kid was hit by a car. Same situation. The rumor was that he had been dating a white girl, and that girl's uncle had hit him late one night, too. But this was before you moved back here."

"Oh, Toni. Don't tell me that! I can't take all of this. I thought Mississippi had changed at least a *little bit* when I went away to college. What are the people in this community doing to stop this kind of thing? Don't tell me that we're going all the way back to this 1950s-type of justice in Mississippi. I didn't move back here to fight the same battles my parents and grandparents had to fight!" Chante could feel her exhaustion threatening to smother her like a damp quilt.

"I know. I know. Are you going to be okay? Do you need me to bring you anything?" Toni asked.

"I just need some time to process all of this."

"Well, just know that the police are supposed to be taking David McKlusky into custody this morning, so it's very likely that you'll be running unopposed from here until election day. I just can't see him trying to finish out this campaign with a murder charge on him for a race crime in a black senatorial district. He's done."

When Chante hung up the phone, she sat on the edge of the bed, unable to move. Everything was happening entirely too fast, and she worried about what she had gotten herself into. This dark, complicated history of Mississippi was the primary reason her parents had moved to Barbados. She, however, had decided to stay, and this was the state that she now called home.

Chante said a silent prayer for Brent Edwards, before crawling back into bed and pulling the covers over her head.

It all seemed surreal. If everything Toni told her was true—and she had no reason to doubt it—then Chante would likely win the election. She should have felt happy and relieved about that, but she didn't.

Then she thought about Grady and wondered how much time he had left. Would his health decline gradually, or would she wake up one morning to hear that he had been taken to a hospital from which he would never return. She dreaded that call, and she found herself watching him so closely at times that she could not avoid living in perpetual fear.

Daily, Mississippi, was supposed to represent life: a new life, new opportunities. But as the sun rose slowly over the small town, the streets seemed to be controlled by the shadows of death.

PART THREE

KEITH LAWRENCE

THE PREVIOUS NOVEMBER, while Keith Lawrence was a sophomore at Daily High School, a black teenager from the junior class was killed in a hit and run accident out in the county. The guy they arrested for the accident claimed he thought he had hit a deer. After all, it was after 1 a.m. and on a dark road in an area where light poles were scarce.

At first the situation appeared to be a legitimate accident. Apparently the kid had been walking along the side of the road and no one could have seen him until the last minute. His body was not discovered until the following morning, and that was only when a curious driver pulled over on the shoulder of the road after seeing what looked like a leg down in a ditch beside the road. The teenager's eyes were half open, his body already beginning to break down from the elements. The most disturbing part of the young man's appearance, however, was the large hole above his brow, a hole that had already begun to fill with water from the early morning drizzle. If that were the end of the story, it would have already been tragic, especially by Daily's standards. But as it turned out, there was more. Much more.

The thirty-something white guy who confessed to accidentally hitting the kid was found to be related to a girl at the high school, a girl who the kid had been supposedly dating. While the police investigation never included any of these details, everyone (especially the black community) knew that the kid's death was no accident.

Keith remembered how his mother had responded: "In this day and age black people are still being lynched!"

He'd flinched when he heard the word "lynched." He thought that was something that happened back in the olden days, but hearing it in reference to the dead student, a person he had known (albeit only in passing), pulled up images his mother had made him look at of a swollen, disfigured Emmit Till propped up in a casket, his remains so soured and decomposed that citizens of Chicago admitted to being able to smell his body from blocks away.

Keith had gone to the kid's wake at the funeral home, just two streets over from his house. Afraid of going alone, he went with Nakeisha Williams, his neighbor from down the street. (Between Keith and Nakeisha, they made up the total population of black teenagers on the integrated side of the railroad tracks.) Nakeisha was Keith's classmate, and the two of them were a year younger than the kid who had been killed.

When they arrived at Gaylord Funeral Home, they stood outside, frozen and unable to step forward. Keith had never seen a dead person who was around his age before, let alone one who had been killed under such suspicious circumstances. He wanted to ask Nakeisha if she had ever seen a dead body before, but he was afraid of sounding too naïve. As they stood there, the sounds of the recorded organ music drifting through the open door, the weight of what they were about to see loomed over them like a roof threatening to cave in.

"I guess we should go in," he finally said.

Nakeisha nodded and lowered her head.

Keith had never been inside of Gaylord Funeral Home, so he was surprised at how short the foyer was —and even more surprised that the viewing room, which didn't appear to have any doors, was clearly visible the moment he walked into the building. He had not expected the immediacy of it all.

He hesitated at the threshold, only moving forward slowly when he saw Nakeisha step forward. Off to the side was a table with an open guestbook. Needing to move away from the open casket that rested against the wall, Keith ambled somberly to the table, lifting the pen that lay across two pages, nearly full of names. He recognized a few of the names, but only the names from Daily High School. He printed his name carefully, using his best penmanship, each letter written so deliberately that it could have been mistaken for a computer generated font: Keith Aaron Lawrence. He put the pen down as slowly as he had picked it up and turned around to find Nakeisha standing in front of the casket, her body obscuring Keith's ability to see anything. Beside the casket was an easel with the deceased's last class photo enlarged, the name beneath it: Antonio Canton. Only when Keith saw the name did the gravity of the situation multiply exponentially. Tony, as Antonio was called by his friends, was known as "Pretty Tony," his light brown skin and wavy hair irresistible to a lot of the girls at the school. Plus, he could sing. He was handsome and talented, a combination that made younger students like Keith look up to him even more.

Pretty Tony.

Keith walked up to stand behind Nakeisha, and when she moved away from the casket, Keith was able to see Pretty Tony for the first time since the "accident." At first, it didn't seem as if he were looking at a real person, definitely not Pretty Tony. Pretty Tony had a light brown complexion; the boy in the casket was at least four shades darker. Pretty Tony had wavy hair; the boy in the casket did not seem to have wavy hair. Maybe this was not Pretty Tony after all. It couldn't be. This boy looked nothing like Pretty Tony—but then there was the mark above his brow, the funeral home's attempt to conceal the hole that had been there. Suddenly Keith found himself staring at the boy's pinched lips and wide nose. Maybe this *was* Pretty Tony, he thought, and then it hit him that he was staring at a guy he had once idolized. That realization took his breath away, and for a moment it seemed as if all of the air had been sucked out of the room. Just as he began to fall over, he caught himself and took a deep breath. He breathed as he looked at Pretty Tony's body. Pretty Tony's body, however, lay still, its last breath having been taken five days ago in a ditch beside a country road.

The spring semester of Keith's sophomore year had been a climb back to normalcy, which was why he so desperately looked forward to the distraction of his comic books and video games when the summer finally arrived. He did not want to admit that he still thought about Pretty Tony and that day at Gaylord Funeral Home. In fact, he wanted to forget it all, but he knew deep down that he never would.

CHAPTER THIRTY-FOUR

THE SUMMER BREAK BEGAN UNEVENTFULLY, which, for Keith, was perfectly fine. He had saved up his allowance and some of the money he received for his birthday a month earlier to purchase the *Monster Rising* graphic novel compendium. He had planned to use a good chunk of his time during the earlier part of the summer break lazily reading the mountainous tome, savoring each page, one at a time.

Keith did not have any other elaborate plans and did not want to interact with any of the students at the school, boy or girl, except for maybe Nakeisha, whom he could not have avoided even if he wanted to. She had grown up down the street from him, and she was his best friend for all intents and purposes, although he rarely thought of her that way. He just knew that she was the person, other than his mother, who knew the most about him and the only person he could entrust with the peculiarities of his fifteen-year-old mind.

If left to his own devices, Keith would have done little more than read comic books, play video games, and occasionally watch a movie, since he had finally convinced his mother to get a Netflix account for the house, but his mother had other plans for his summer.

When she walked into the room holding a copy of Toni Morrison's *Song of Solomon*, Keith began to feel the dread that often accompanied the moment his mother would bring in a book she wanted him to read. That was one of the downsides to having a mother who held a PhD in African-American literature, with a dissertation centered around Toni Morrison: you were always expected to read some incredibly difficult book and be prepared to discuss it and maybe even write a paper on it. Sometimes Keith wondered if his mother was confusing him with one of her students over at State University. Those people were paying for the privilege of reading those dense texts, not he. Keith had other more pressing things on his mind than pretending to be older than he was. The *Monster Rising* compendium was one of them.

"You're going to read this book this summer," she said, placing the book on the bed beside him.

"But, Mom, do I have to?"

"I don't know how you could even fix your mouth to ask me that question. You have the complete summer ahead of you, and I haven't heard you say that you're going to do anything productive with it. So I'm going to help you make it productive. Read the book, Keith."

Keith started to pout, but knew better. His mother didn't play that game. Because his father died when he was two years old, much too young for Keith to have any real memories of the man, he had always known his mother to overcompensate for the absence. When she laid down the law, he had little choice but to abide.

Sometimes he wondered if his father were still alive would his mother be this way. Would she be the kind of strict and demanding parent that she'd become? At the time of his father's death, his mother was halfway through her masters degree. Keith imagined that it must have been difficult for her, being in school and having a son to look after. Having to do all of these things by herself had to have shaped the kind of woman she'd become.

He didn't mind, though. He loved that his mother was firm, and it was cool telling his friends at school that his mother was a professor at the local university and that he came from a smart family. But sometimes it could all be too much. Any other summer he would have had no problem taking on her reading assignment, but after the school year he'd just finished, he wanted only to relax and clear his head.

He had wrestled with Pretty Tony's death more than he'd expected. The fact that one of his classmates could be killed by another human being, just because he was black was difficult for Keith to accept. After being unable to sleep for several nights, he broke down and told his mother what had been troubling him. He didn't know what he expected his mother to say or do, as she was not the overly affectionate type, but he didn't expect the response he received.

"Keith, the universe bends towards justice. That's what Martin Luther King, Jr. said."

He had expected her to give him a talk wrapped in spiritual overtones, maybe hold him close to her and whisper about how much she loved him and would never allow something like that to ever happen to him. No. She had instead given him a quote, and that quote had been delivered in such a detached way that it were as if her emotional center were completely unavailable —and that hurt his feelings. At times he even felt that he hated her for it, but she was all that he had, and he knew his mother was probably a different person when his father had been alive. He had to cut her more slack, he knew.

So Toni Morrison it was. If that would make his mother happy, then that's exactly what he would do.

## CHAPTER THIRTY-FIVE

KEITH ATTEMPTED to start Toni Morrison's *Song of Solomon* three times before realizing he just wasn't ready to apply the kind of focus to the text necessary to understand what she was talking about. He had always heard Toni Morrison was one of the more difficult writers to read, especially if you preferred the much easier to follow commercial fiction that filled that aisles of Wal-Mart and the local grocery stores. Even the solitary bookstore (that was not a Christian bookstore) kept Toni Morrison's books away from the front of the store and in the section designated "Literature" so as to not scare, Keith figured, the legions of fans looking for the more fast-paced, bestselling thrillers.

His mind was elsewhere anyway. He was making serious progress with the *Monster Rising* compendium, which was composed of the first ten graphic novels built around the first sixty-three issues of what had quickly become his first favorite comic book since he had begun his long and wonderfully exciting trek through the world that Image Comics gift wrapped to fanboys the country over: *The Walking Dead*. *Monster Rising* was the story of the United States in the near future, a place where a league of marine animals—monsters!—were emerging from the depths of the ocean due to climate change. A lot of these animals, which up until that point had never been identified by marine biologists, died as they rose from the dark depths of the ocean, but the few that survived and adapted found their way into strained interactions with human beings. While the book was not a zombie book like *The Walking Dead*, it did have a feeling of the "undead" emerging from the murky waters of the world with a serious appetite for humans. Keith had read that a television show was in development and decided that he would read every issue before episode one was televised.

But then his mother had brought him Toni Morrison to read.

After a few false starts, Keith simply realized that he needed to finish the compendium even faster than he had planned if he wanted to meet his mother's deadline, because there was no way he could get his brain to process the suicide from atop Mercy Hospital that opens *Song of Solomon* when all he could think about was whether the small crew of Americans still living on a half-submerged continent (that climate change was a bitch!) could fight off the twelve whale-sized monsters who ate human beings like Tic-Tacs.

Keith wondered briefly if Nakeisha had ever read anything by Toni Morrison. She was always reading really thick books written by all of those dead authors that the English teachers loved so much. She was also the smartest friend he had. While Keith was slow to publicly admit it, he thought she was also very pretty, which was probably the reason she didn't catch much flack at Daily High School for being so bookish. The other girls apparently didn't feel threatened by a girl who would rather read a book than walk around switching her ass in front of boys while wearing shorts that were so short a girl could catch a yeast infection just by bending over to tie her shoes. If Nakeisha had read Toni Morrison's *Song of Solomon*, Keith knew he might be able to finish the book much faster (yes, he would still need to read it, but he could ask questions along the way, thereby slowing down the amount of time it took to not just read, but to understand, what the hell was going on in the book). He would call her that afternoon once he'd finished his errands for the day. Hopefully she could help him, because at this rate, he knew he would be in trouble with his mother for failing his summer reading assignment.

## CHAPTER THIRTY-SIX

"OF COURSE I've read *Song of Solomon*!"

Hearing Nakeisha say this was music to Keith's ears. He couldn't help but ask, "So can you tell me what it's about?"

"It is about a guy named Milkman and how he deals with his family's history."

Keith twisted his eyebrows. "What does that even mean?"

Nakeisha laughed. "You'll just have to read it. Toni Morrison has a really unique way of telling stories."

"So you can't give me like the *Cliff's Notes* version of the story?"

"Why?" Nakeisha asked, her curiosity piqued.

Keith adjusted his back against the front steps of Nakeisha's house in an effort to alleviate some of the awkwardness of the steps' edges digging into his back. "My mom wants me to read the book this summer, and I just can't seem to get into it. I'm knee deep into the *Monster Rising* compendium, and I can't get my mind focused enough for Toni Morrison."

Nakeisha took a bite of some grapes from a bowl

on her lap. "I wish I could help you on that one. You could always google a synopsis."

"I tried that, but what I saw online didn't make much sense either."

"I can see why. That book wasn't written to be diced up into a cheat sheet."

"Whatever."

"Don't get an attitude with me, Mr. I-Don't-Want-to-Read-a-Book-I'm-Supposed-to-Read," she said, laughing.

"I'm going to start it soon. I was just hoping I could make it past the first three pages without feeling like I was stupid."

"I wish I could tell you more about the beginning of the book, but that plays into what happens later on. I wouldn't want to spoil it for you." Nakeisha took another bite of her grapes. "It's a really good book, Keith. Trust me. And it's easier to follow than some of her other books."

"Well, I only plan to read this one."

"I'm curious, but why does your mom make you read these kinds of books every summer?"

"Because she's an African-American lit professor at State University. She probably gets her kicks by forcing me to read this kind of stuff. Plus, she did her dissertation on Toni Morrison. She's like a Toni Morrison fiend. She belongs to the Toni Morrison Society and even has a local group she put together to discuss those books. I don't get it, but that's just the way she is."

"That's not a bad way to be, though. I would love to have a job where I could talk about great books all day," Nakeisha said.

"Well, maybe she should adopt you and your mom should adopt me."

Nakeisha laughed. "Don't tempt me."

"So do you have any tips on how to get started with this book?" Keith asked.

Nakeisha looked upward, as if pondering the question for a moment. "I don't really know," she responded. "I guess you have to look at Toni Morrison's writing like you're jumping rope, double-dutch style."

"What do you mean?" Keith said.

"It's kind of like Toni Morrison is throwing the ropes fast from both hands."

"You're starting to lose me here," Keith said, exasperated.

"Okay," Nakeisha said, adjusting herself and moving the bowl of grapes out of her way. She looked as if she were preparing to try again. "Have you ever jumped rope?"

Keith knew the answer to that question, but he was unsure if he wanted to admit that he knew how to do something that was supposedly a "girl" activity. His cousin Portia had taught him how to do it years earlier when he was just a little kid, but he had stopped doing it altogether when a group of boys across the street from Portia's house in Chicago started making fun of him by calling him a "sissy." Embarrassed, he had created a gulf of distance between the activity of jumping rope (along with any other activity traditionally associated with girls) and the masculine demeanor he had wanted to project. Even at that very young age, he knew that whatever names your peers gave you could stick to you like a super adhesive wood bonding glue. The fact that he had an uncle they still called Wee-Wee, although Wee-Wee was now in his forties, was proof positive that you could not necessarily outgrow some unfortunate childhood names, whether they were caused by someone hoping to come off as being clever, someone trying to be funny, or someone refusing to let up on another person and committing himself to making sure that a ridiculed person never forgot a particular unfortunate childhood incident. So Nakeisha's question fell flat on the floor for a moment before Keith finally responded, "Say that I did know what you were talking about."

"What about double-dutching? Should I *assume* that you know how to do that one, too?" she asked.

Caught in his attempt to dodge her question, Keith could only nod through his embarrassment.

"As you *might* already know, double-dutch jump roping is all about timing. If you can see how the ropes are falling just so, you can dive right in. But if your timing is off, then the ropes hit you, tangle up, and drop to the ground. That's just like the way it is with Toni Morrison. You have to catch the style she is writing with and dive right in, jumping in between the words."

Keith laughed. "Damn, you sound just like my mother. You should definitely become a college professor one day."

"I want to be a writer. Just a writer."

"I feel you." He didn't want to bust Nakeisha's bubble, but Keith's mother had always warned him of the jobs that made little to no money, and being a writer was at the top of the list. He had often wondered if his mother had only said that because she had never gotten any publishers to consider publishing her second critical study of Toni Morrison's work.

"So try to get into her writing from the first sentence. Bear down and don't let up. It'll all make sense in the end. You have to trust her on that. You know that she has a Nobel Prize in Literature, right? I would definitely trust her if I were you," Nakeisha said.

"Well can I come to you to talk about this book if I have any questions?" Keith asked.

"Sure," she responded.

"Cool."

The two of them sat on the steps of her house in silence, staring out ahead of them at the house across the street. It looked very similar to the architecture of the other houses on that street: one level brick houses that were elevated above the ground enough to have low steps (like the ones Keith and Nakeisha were now lying on). The house's wooden trim along the base of the roof, however, was a smurf blue, which made the house both unique and fun to look at, especially since the people who lived there, the Richardsons, were hardly ever there due to the fact that they were an elderly white couple known for spending their time traveling from state to state, visiting their children and grandchildren. The Richardsons had even once asked if Keith and Nakeisha could keep an eye on their house while they were away. As a result, Keith and Nakeisha found themselves unconsciously looking at the Richardsons' house every day since, out of both habit and the need to have a focal point for their eyes while they daydreamed about their futures, futures that both hoped would one day take them away from Daily.

"You like movies?" Nakeisha finally asked.

"You already know the answer to that question," he responded, smiling. "I'm a film junky. I might even go on to film school one day. I'm dead serious."

"That's nice," Nakeisha responded, almost too carefully. "Maybe we could go and catch a movie together some time."

"That sounds cool. There're supposed to be a few superhero movies coming out his summer. Are you into superhero movies?" he asked.

"Sure."

"Are you a DC fangirl, a Marvel fangirl, or do you do indies?"

Nakeisha's eyes widened as if she didn't entirely understand the question.

"You know. Do you like Batman and Superman and Wonder Woman? They're with the DC comic book universe. Spiderman and Thor and Iron Man and Captain America are all a part of the Marvel universe. And *The Walking Dead*, that show on AMC, is based off of the Image comic book series."

"Well, I can say this much: you know a lot more about superheroes that I do. I just like seeing a good movie, especially if I have good company."

"I'm definitely down with you if you're trying to go and catch any of the ones coming out this summer. Just let me know when."

"When is the next movie?"

"I think they have something coming out this Friday, but I have to check."

"Okay. So how about this Friday then?"

"That's cool," Keith said.

As Keith got up to leave, he noticed a smile on Nakeisha's face that had not been there before. It was only then that he realized that he might have just agreed to go on a date with his best friend.

CHAPTER THIRTY-SEVEN

KEITH HAD GOTTEN HIS "INTERMEDIATE" license, the odd duck of Mississippi driver's licenses, a few months earlier. The intermediate license meant that he had to be off the road by 10:00 p.m., unless there was a driver 21-years-old or older riding along in the passenger seat. Since he and Nakeisha were the same age, he knew they would have to catch the early show.

There were two cars at his house: the newer Jeep Grand Cherokee, decked out with a sweet wraparound grille guard, and the old manual transmission Volkswagen Jetta that had clearly seen better days. His mother had given him the older of the two vehicles. He mainly used it to drive to and from school. He had never taken a girl out on a date, and he was unsure if taking Nakeisha to the movies would qualify as one.

Did *she* think it was a date? That was the real question.

He replayed everything they had said to each other and was still unsure about what was going on.

He guessed that the more interesting question was did she actually like him? He hadn't given much thought as to how he felt about her, but now it was on his mind in the heaviest of ways.

He knew that he found her cute, but they were just friends, right? She knew far too much about him for him to like her in a romantic way. That would be too weird—like trying to date your "play" sister.

He started to call her and ask her what was up, but he was too nervous. What if she clowned him for making such an assumption? He didn't think he could live down the embarrassment of her qualifying their relationship to each other as platonic. It would make him feel stupid, and the one thing he dreaded most was coming across as stupid in front of a girl as smart as Nakeisha.

Friday arrived slowly, in the absence of school. He was desperate to go out and do something, too. He was starting to make some serious headway on *Song of Solomon* and was rather proud of himself for making it through the first sixty pages. Things were finally starting to make some sense.

Not knowing how to dress for this "outing" with Nakeisha, he tossed on a lightweight short-sleeve cotton button-up, a pair of khaki cargo shorts and a pair of casual sneakers. He was preppy enough, without drawing too much suspicion that he was attempting to impress her. He didn't know how he had gotten this far in his thoughts of her. He was reluctant to admit that he liked her and had settled on the idea that he was open to whatever went down. He would leave it all in her hands. If she expressed any interest, he would jump on it like a starved dog on a bone, but if she kept it straight-up platonic, he would smile it off and keep things status quo.

While Keith could have easily walked down the

street to pick her up, he opted to drive the Jetta down the street and park it in her driveway.

"Look at you!" Nakeisha said, opening the door. "You're looking like a little cutie."

"Really?" he said, before reciprocating with his own compliment of her cream colored sundress. She even smelled like sexy fruit. (Was that really a thing?)

"Thank you," she said, standing in the doorway. "Come on in, and I'll be ready in a few minutes. What time does our movie start?"

"5:30." He glanced at the clock on the wall behind her and noticed that it was 4:15. Because there was no movie theater in Daily, they would have to drive to the next town over. He had calculated all of this into the time he gave her to be ready. If they arrived early, maybe they could chill out somewhere and talk before the movie started.

"So how is it going with your book?" Nakeisha called out from one of the rooms adjacent to the den.

"Not bad. I'm finally making some progress. You should have told me how strange the book is, though."

She laughed. "I didn't want to take away the fun."

"Dude nursing off his mama's breast, his ass so big his feet are flat on the damn floor. Come on. His aunt doesn't have a freaking belly button! He's doing his own cousin? That book is crazy."

"Everything I've read by Toni Morrison has something in there that flirts with being just this side of crazy," Nakeisha said, walking back into the room.

With her lip gloss and circular sunglasses, she looked like a woman clearly going on a date. This made Keith smile.

"Ready?" she asked.

"Sure."

As he walked her around to the passenger side of

the car and opened the door for her, he quietly rejoiced when he saw her lean over and pop open his door in return.

He didn't know if this was a date, but he was going to treat it as if it were.

Cranking up the car, he looked over at Nakeisha and smiled. She chuckled at him and playfully poked his arm. "Boy, you so crazy!"

THE MOVIE WAS GOOD, but not as good as the company. The movie lasted just over two hours, and Keith and Nakeisha sat all the way through the credits, at Keith's suggestion, to get a teaser for the next superhero movie due out later that summer.

On the way to the car, they talked about the movie and how much they enjoyed it, Keith going on and on about the comic book universe out of which the movie had come. He had expected her to think it was all corny, but she was just as enthusiastic about the movie as he had been. They decided to grab a bite to eat at a restaurant down the street from the theater, and by the time they were seated, Keith assumed that this was indeed a date after all.

"So how are you planning on spending your summer?" he asked, as they picked at the nacho appetizer they had ordered.

"I guess just chilling out around Daily, reading and getting a jumpstart on the school year."

"Seriously? We just finished school and you're making up homework for yourself already?"

"So says the guy who is reading Toni Morrison during his summer break."

"Touché."

He was actually glad that Nakeisha was going to be around over the summer. At least now he wouldn't be alone.

"I'm thinking about helping out with the election, though," she added.

"Doing what?"

"You know this is the first election in the history of Humma County where there is a black person running for every office on the ballot, don't you?" Nakeisha said rhetorically. "There's a woman named Chante House running for the new senate seat, and I plan on going by her headquarters some time next week to see what I can do to help out with her campaign."

Keith dipped another nacho. "Why *her* campaign?"

"She's actually the only black woman on the ballot, and I want to do all I can to help her get elected. I know we're too young to vote, but we can still make a difference in this election."

Keith nodded, "True. You must be planning to major in political science when you go to college."

"Either that or English. I still don't know. Maybe I'll do a double major."

Keith's eyes widened. "Double major? I'd be lucky to find one major that I could commit to. What schools are you thinking about applying to?"

"Ellison-Wright, Spelman, Hampton, or Howard."

"Aren't those all black colleges?"

"Yep."

The server arrived with their dinner orders, and for a moment, they ate in silence, before Keith asked, "Why are you only applying to black colleges? We're in the new millennium. I'm surprised that there are still any black colleges around for people to apply to."

Nakeisha put down her fork and rolled her eyes. "I can't believe you just said something as ignorant as that. There's just as much of a need for Historically Black Colleges and Universities as there's ever been. Did you know most black professionals and PhDs started at black colleges? Black colleges are the shit!"

"Well, okay," Keith said, feeling bad about his comment. He didn't know much about black colleges, and the university his mother taught at was predominately white. He figured that it made more sense for him to go to a school that was more reflective of the world he knew. "I'm just saying that someone as smart as you could be going to Harvard or Stanford or some place like that."

"Black colleges are doing amazing things these days. Did you know that they produce Rhodes Scholars and their alumni go on to do amazing things in various industries? Shoot, Hampton University has the largest proton therapy beam cancer treatment center in the country."

"What in the world is a proton therapy beam?"

"It's a radiation beam that doctors can use to target cancer cells without causing harm to healthy cells. I read about it online."

Keith chuckled. "You sound like a brochure or something."

Nakeisha's face became serious. "There's nothing funny about black colleges, and to be honest, Keith, after living in this racist-ass town, I need a break. I want to be free to learn without worrying about some white man trying to run me or my friends down with his car."

There it was. Pretty Tony. Keith had tried to bury

the memory of that day in the funeral home in the back of his mind, but now it was released to the surface. He didn't know what to say, so he lowered his head and continued eating.

"Don't tell me you don't think about what happened to Pretty Tony when you think about Daily. I seriously doubt I will stick around here next summer. The colleges I'm looking to apply to all have summer programs for rising seniors, and I plan on taking advantage of one of them."

"Okay," Keith said, still unable to center his thoughts.

The ride back to Daily was quiet, with only the soft music of the radio playing in the background.

When Keith pulled up to Nakeisha's house at 9:30, he still had not said a word. He turned off the car.

"What's on your mind?" she asked.

"I don't know. You just put a lot of stuff on my mind at dinner."

"Stuff like what?"

"Pretty Tony and what-not. I guess I thought I was over it, but, well, you know."

Nakeisha nodded. "I didn't mean to put a damper on the evening. I really had a lot of fun going out with you. I guess sometimes I get carried away and say too much. I just get tired of people dissing black colleges, and the main ones who are dissing them don't know a damn thing about them."

Keith nodded. "Well, I'm sorry. I didn't mean anything by what I said."

Nakeisha said, "You know it doesn't even have to be like that. We go way back, and we had a good time tonight, didn't we? I know I did."

"Yeah, I had a good time."

"Well, let's not let one disagreement spoil the evening."

Keith smiled. "So there's something I've been meaning to ask you all evening."

"What's that?"

"Was this a date?"

"I don't know. Was it?"

"It felt like a date," he responded.

"Well, what would you do at the end of a date once you've gotten your date home?"

Keith blushed, unable to conceal his smile. "I guess I'd do this," he said, leaning over and kissing Nakeisha gently on her lips. He expected her to dodge him at first, but when she didn't, he settled into the beauty of the moment and everything else became a memory.

## CHAPTER THIRTY-NINE

TWO DAYS AFTER THE DATE, Keith couldn't stop thinking about Nakeisha. They had actually kissed! They were no longer just friends, at least in his mind. He knew she wasn't his girlfriend, per se, but he definitely saw the potential for that to happen soon.

As he sat on the edge of his bed, placing down his copy of *Song of Solomon*, he checked his vibrating phone for the incoming text.

*RU ready to go over?*

He typed, "Yep."

He locked up the house, hopped in the Jetta, and headed down to Nakeisha's house.

She came bounding out as soon as he arrived. She was wearing a pair of neat khakis and a starched blouse.

"Am I underdressed?" Keith said, looking down at his t-shirt and basketball shorts.

"Not really," Nakeisha responded, as he opened her door for her and she thanked him.

"But you look like you're going some place important."

"I am. *We* are. We're going to help the first black

woman get elected to the senate from Humma County."

"Okay. Well, I should definitely change then."

"Keith, we don't have time for all of that. Let's just go."

"Are they expecting us at a particular time?"

"Not exactly."

"Well, let's drop by my house for a quick sec, and I'll change. At least we can look like we both mean business and not just one of us."

Nakeisha sighed. "Okay, but you have to be quick about it. I'm really excited about meeting her. She's my new shero."

"What's a shero?"

"She-ro, like hero."

"Oh. I get it. Cool."

They backed out of her driveway and within seconds they were in his own.

"Wanna come in?" he said. "The AC is funny in this old car, and I don't want you to burn up out here. It really only kicks on when the car is in motion. Go figure."

Nakeisha stepped out of the car and patted her clothes to make sure they weren't wrinkled. She then followed him into the house.

"I'm really making some progress with the novel. In fact, I'm thinking I might be able to finish it in another week or so. I'm even understanding most of what I'm reading. I just have a question."

Nakeisha walked casually around his room, glancing at the posters of Outkast and Big K.R.I.T., alongside the posters of Miles Davis and John Coltrane. "What's your question?"

He reached in his closet and removed one of the pre-ironed short sleeve button-up shirts hanging there.

He liked to run heat on his clothes as soon as they came out of the dryer so he wouldn't have to do it later. Pulling off his t-shirt, he said, "If the Seven Days are all about doing some Code of Hammurabi 'eye for an eye' shit, then why would they go after a black dude? I thought they were all about paying back white people for all the sick, racist shit they did to black people."

Nakeisha looked at him for a second, and he noticed she was looking at his chest. She quickly responded, "I think the Seven Days going after Milkman was more personal than the usual stuff they did."

He smiled. He liked the way she was trying to check him out on the sly. Just for the fun of it, he tightened his abs and flexed his arms. "Welcome to the…"

"Don't say it," she started.

"Gun show, baby!"

"Damn. You really just said that."

He pulled on his shirt quickly and buttoned it, laughing. "You can say it. I know I need to put on some weight. I'm like the skinniest guy in the gym. I'm no Brent Edwards." The more he talked about his physique, the more self-conscious he became.

"Stop it, Keith."

"What?"

"Stop saying those things about yourself. I think your body is very nice."

"Really?"

"You might be thin, but you're pretty cut. I think that's sexy."

Keith smiled. That was the first time that she had ever used that word when referring to him.

He walked over to her and lifted her chin so that their lips met. "You're beautiful," he said, kissing her again.

She looked at him, her eyes seeming to take all of him in, then closed them, leaning into his kiss.

Keith expected her to push back after a while, but she seemed quite content to be close to him, feeling their bodies pressed together. When her fingernails lightly brushed down his back, he felt himself want more than just a kiss. He began backing her slowly toward his bed.

She sat down, staring up at him as he unbuttoned his shirt. "Keith, where's your mom?"

"She's over at the university. She's usually there most of the day, teaching summer school classes and doing research in the library. It's cool. She's a town away."

As Keith knelt before her, she pealed back his shirt, exposing his chest. "I just want to touch you, but I don't want us to have sex, okay?"

He nodded. "Sure. Touching is fine with me."

Nakeisha ran her fingers along the warm skin of his chest, stomach, and arms. "Have you ever done it before?"

"Yeah," he said, lying, before thinking about it and correcting himself. "No. I haven't. I'm like the only dude I know who's a virgin."

"That's not a bad thing," she responded. "Most of these boys are so nasty because they mess with nasty girls. That's why I'm a virgin, too."

Keith sighed, relieved. "I like that."

Nakeisha smiled and leaned forward kissing his chest lightly.

He carefully unbuttoned her shirt and admired the firmness of her body. Her bra was black, but he could tell it was slightly cushioned. He moved forward to slide one of the cups upward.

"They're kind of small," she said, moving her arm across her chest.

"They're just fine. Beautiful, just like you."

She moved her arm and allowed him to remove her bra. Taking her hand, Keith lifted her from the bed and into his warm embrace. Their chests touching, they kissed and held onto each other.

"I could stand here with you all day."

"So could I," Nakeisha said.

He reached down to unbutton her pants, and she blocked him with her hand. "No. I don't want to go there. Not yet."

"Okay," Keith managed.

"It's all right, baby," she said, kissing him again. "Let's go slow. Can we go slow?"

His frustration gave way to a smile. "Sure."

The truth was that he wanted to enjoy every step of the way with Nakeisha. After all, they had been friends for a long time, and there was no need to rush. Neither one of them was going anywhere.

"We should probably go over to Chante House's office, right?" she said.

"Sure."

They both watched the other as they adjusted their clothing.

"Let's go help your shero get elected," Keith said, following Nakeisha out of the room.

## CHAPTER FORTY

KEITH HADN'T EXPECTED Chante House to be so attractive. When Nakeisha had mentioned her to him, he had assumed Chante would be an older woman, not unlike his mother. Instead, she had the air of a person who was destined to be famous, even if that was just *Southern* famous.

Nakeisha did most of the talking, and while they only had a few minutes to speak with Chante, it was clear they had picked the right candidate to support. She was smart, beautiful, articulate, and purely about business. Keith made it up in his mind to talk to his mother that evening about putting one of Chante's yard signs in the front yard.

Chante had then turned them over to her campaign manager, a woman who, as far as Keith was concerned, looked more like what he had expected Chante to look like. The woman, Toni Savage, was sharply dressed, but in the right kind of light, she had a dude-like swagger to her, Keith noticed.

Their first assignment was to canvas their own neighborhood with campaign literature, and they had eagerly agreed.

Leaving the office building, he looked over at Nakeisha. "So what was it like meeting yourself in ten years?"

She chuckled lightly. "If I'm like her in ten years, I will consider myself extremely lucky."

Taking her hand and kissing it, he said, "I believe you'll be there, plus some. Trust me."

## CHAPTER FORTY-ONE

KEITH AND NAKEISHA blazed through their neighborhood, knocking on doors and then handing their neighbors information cards and flyers about Chante House. Once they made the block, Nakeisha said, "Why don't we walk down Main Street and hand out some of the rest of these?"

Keith was feeling pretty good about what they had accomplished and was ready to go do something else. After all, they had only been asked to canvass their neighborhood. There was no point in doing more than what was asked of them. Still, he liked walking and talking with Nakeisha as they moved from house to house, so he agreed. "We can hit the houses along Main Street and make the block back around to this street." He knew Main Street was full of antebellum houses of white people who didn't too much associate with black people, but at least the walk back around to their street would take them through a black neighborhood.

The first two houses they knocked on had no cars in the driveways, so they left flyers in the grooves of the closed doors. By the time they reached the third house, the absence of people started to appear somewhat suspicious.

"I'm starting to think there are people in these houses, and they just don't want to come to the door," Keith said.

"I was thinking the same thing. Why don't we just finish up this strip and head on back around."

Keith nodded. "Sounds like a plan."

As they walked up the path to the door of the last antebellum house, Keith noticed someone moving past the window. "I just saw someone."

"So someone should answer the door then," Nakeisha said.

"Let's hope so."

Keith reached over and pushed the doorbell. The sound of chimes echoed throughout the house from behind the door.

They waited patiently, and when no one answered, he pushed the doorbell again.

The door opened so quickly it startled them.

"Get off my property!" an old white man yelled. "You're trespassing. Now gon' and git!"

"Sir," Nakeisha said, holding out a flyer to him. "We just wanted to give you…"

"If you don't get your black asses off my property, I am entitled to defend myself."

Keith placed an arm across Nakeisha and carefully backed away, easing her back at the same time. "There's no need for that, sir."

The old man cracked open the door, and a rifle was visible alongside his leg.

Keith's heart felt as if it would beat out of his chest, but he kept easing backward, Nakeisha's hand interlocked with his own. When they returned to the sidewalk, the old man closed the door.

"Oh my god!" Nakeisha started. "He was going to shoot us!"

"I think he just wanted to scare us."

"Now do you see, Keith? Now do you see why I want to leave this town?" Her voice was shaky, and he sensed that she might be on the verge of crying.

He quickly pulled her close to him, and she embraced him.

"Fuck him," Keith said, still shaken himself. "Let's just head home."

They turned down a side street that ran them into a predominately black neighborhood. Kids were in the streets throwing footballs back and forth or jumping rope. One kid was staring at his cell phone screen while eating a popsicle.

Keith figured the kids enjoying the summer afternoon around them had to lift Nakeisha's spirits. He looked at her and smiled. She smiled in return.

"Want to hand out any more flyers or just call it a day?" he asked.

"You know what?" she said. "I refuse to let one racist cracker mess up my day. Chante House probably has to deal with a lot more than what we just did."

Keith wanted to say, "But she signed up for this. We didn't." Instead, he nodded his agreement.

Nakeisha pointed to a house a few feet away. "That's Ms. Jenkins's house over there. She used to work at the school cafeteria before she went on disability. Let's see if she'll agree to take a yard sign."

While they didn't have any yard signs with them, one of the things Toni Savage had told them to do was identify well-positioned yards and see if the owners of those homes would be willing to put up a Chante House for State Senate sign. If the owner agreed, Keith and Nakeisha were to let Toni know and she would send someone around with a sign later on.

As they approached the squat one-level brick house, they could see two small children sitting under the carport, one sucking her thumb, the other licking some powdered confection out of his palm. Nakeisha waved to the children, and they just stared at her, thumb in mouth, palm to face.

Keith pushed the doorbell, although the wooden door behind the outer glass door was wide open.

"Y'all come on in," Ms. Jenkins said, waving them in from her couch.

They walked into the house slowly, and the first thing Keith noticed was all the plastic covering the furniture in the room.

"Close that door! Y'all lettin' all of the air out!"

Nakeisha quickly closed the door. "Sorry, Ms. Jenkins."

"How y'all doin'?" the old woman asked.

"Fine, ma'am," they responded, almost in unison.

Ms. Jenkins had to have been well over two hundred pounds, and the way in which she was propped up on the couch made her look even larger. Toys littered the floor and there were several plates on the coffee table, each containing the dried remains of food and sauces. The place reminded Keith of the slave den of the Wicked Witch of the West in the movie *The Wiz*. He wondered if he threw water on Ms. Jenkins would she melt like Mable King's character had.

"What can I do y'all for?"

"Ms. Jenkins, we just wanted to drop off this flyer for Attorney Chante House. She's running for state senator. We would appreciate your vote."

Ms. Jenkins eyed them suspiciously. "She got y'all out here campaigning for her?"

"We volunteered, ma'am," Nakeisha said. "Attorney House has a chance to make history, and we would appreciate your vote."

"I ain't votin', and if I did, I wouldn't vote for her."

Keith looked at Nakeisha trying to gage her reaction.

"Why not?" Nakeisha asked.

"I don't vote for folks that ain't right with the Lord."

Keith had been silent up to this point, but he could no longer sit quietly while this strange old lady dissed Nakeisha's role model.

"What do you mean?" he asked.

"She and that bull dagger need to get right with God before she try to run for somethin'."

"What are you even talking about?" Keith responded.

"Y'all out here knocking on doors for folks that be doin' the Devil's work."

Nakeisha seemed to swell up with anger. "Don't say that, Ms. Jenkins. That's not true." Her voice was steady but firm. "Attorney House is a good person, and she will make a great senator, with or without your vote."

Before Keith knew it, Nakeisha had turned around and was already out the door. He quickly followed behind her.

"Nakeisha, wait up!" he called to her, but she was already storming down the street. He had to jog to catch up to her.

"That old woman is crazy!" she yelled to no one in particular.

"Keisha, calm down. It's not that serious. You know how some people are."

"I swear. If it's not one thing, it's another. Racist

white people. Ignorant black people. What's the point? Why do I even bother?"

Keith didn't know what to say. He felt the same as Nakeisha, and he understood why everything bothered her. That was just the nature of living in Daily, he figured. He was used to it, and a part of him was surprised that at this stage in her life Nakeisha wasn't used to it, too.

He didn't think Chante House was gay, but he knew that Toni Savage was. Even Stevie Wonder could have seen that. Still, it didn't really matter either way. His mother always talked about how all people needed to be treated fairly and that some people liked to use religion as an excuse to say or do whatever they wanted. He imagined that was because she had done all of that graduate work on slave narratives for her masters degree and how she told him that white people had used religion to keep black folks in check. Maybe that's why that dude Solomon from *Song of Solomon* had flown away to Africa—or why that other dude from the beginning of the novel tried to fly off the roof of the hospital.

If only we all had wings, Keith thought, as he wrapped his arm around Nakeisha's shoulders.

They walked home in silence.

## CHAPTER FORTY-TWO

WHEN THEY MADE it back to Nakeisha's house, she told Keith that she wasn't feeling well and that she wanted to lie down. He tried to convince her that having him around might lighten her mood, but after a while, he figured that she might be right. Maybe she did need some time to herself. That was something he knew about his mother: sometimes a person just needed some time alone.

Even though his father had passed away thirteen years ago, Keith's mother would still occasionally drift into a melancholic state and need some time to herself. During those moments, she would close her door and turn on Donny Hathaway's "A Song For You." That had to have been the saddest song Keith had ever heard, and he didn't know if that was because of his mother or because of the song itself, with its haunting melody and Donny Hathaway's tragic backstory.

Keith walked the short distance to his house and was surprised to see his mother's Grand Cherokee in the driveway. He thought he had memorized her work schedule for the summer, but seeing her vehicle startled him. What if she had walked in on him and Nakeisha earlier? She would have definitely lit into him. While he knew that his mother was fond of Nakeisha, he also knew that you couldn't get caught making out with your girl in your room, while playing the odds of not getting caught.

"Mom?" he called out as he entered the foyer. "Mom?"

"In my office," she called back.

Because they lived in a four-bedroom house, his mother had converted the smallest of the rooms into her personal home office, while leaving a guest room, and a room apiece for her and Keith.

Keith walked up to the doorway of his mother's office and found her hunched over her desk looking at a book. "Can I come in?" he asked.

"Sure."

He walked up to his mother, leaned down and kissed her cheek, then stood over her shoulder looking at the book opened before her. Lynchings of black people filled the pages, and the sight of so many deaths captured on only two pages startled him for a moment.

"Mom, why are you looking at that?"

She continued turning pages of the book slowly, examining more pictures of lynchings. "I don't want to ever forget. I don't want *us* to ever forget. This is what they do to you in this state if you're not careful."

The matter-of-fact way in which his mother said the words scared him.

He continued watching her in silence and considered telling her about his and Nakeisha's brush with that white man who had the gun. He didn't want to compound the emotions he knew his mother must have been experiencing, so he decided to keep it to himself.

"Did you finish the novel?"

"Huh?" he said, suddenly aware that his mother was now speaking to him.

"Did you finish *Song of Solomon*?" she asked again.

"Yes, ma'am."

"Good."

She closed the book on her desk and then stood up. She patted him on his shoulder in a somewhat detached way and again said, "Good."

She left him alone in her office, confused.

## CHAPTER FORTY-THREE

KEITH COULD HEAR the sounds of Donny Hathaway creeping from behind the walls of his mother's bedroom door. He placed his hand against the wood and considered knocking, but he knew she needed that moment to herself.

He went to his own room and lay on the bed, staring at the ceiling above him. He wondered what his father had been like—and even more, he wondered what his mother had been like with his father. He closed his eyes and tried to imagine his mother as a happy person, not the strict and sometimes distant woman who occasionally gave him glimpses of a maternal self.

He reached over and grabbed his dogged copy of *Song of Solomon* off his nightstand. His mother didn't seem at all interested in quizzing him about the book or even having him write an essay on it like she had with the other books she had forced upon him in the past. What was so special about this book? He had finished it and thought that the book was pretty good, but he sensed his mother might have viewed it differently than he had. To him, it was just a well-written book, entertaining and full of a wealth of material one could write on for days, but it was just a book. He sensed that it was more than that to his mother, and he just wanted to understand why.

This was normally when he would have called Nakeisha, just to hear a friendly voice, but he knew she needed her space as well.

What was it with the women in his life? Was it possible everyone needed space at the exact same time on the exact same day? If racism were a living and breathing person, he (or she) would likely be the one to blame, but in its absence, the hate was just another molecule in the air of Daily. Maybe they all breathed it and it just affected different people in different ways.

Maybe it was a deep breath of that hate that caused Pretty Tony to get killed.

Nakeisha had a plan, though. She was leaving Daily the first chance she got. Keith wanted to leave, too, but his plan was not as defined as hers. Then he realized that their departures could easily take them in totally different directions. Maybe she would move to Atlanta or Hampton or Washington, DC. He didn't know where he would end up, but it seemed as though, whatever happened, they would be apart from each other. They had always been neighbors, and he could count on a single hand the days he had not seen or spoken to her. If they were to be separated due to their desires to escape Daily, he didn't want their relationship to be yet another casualty of those hate molecules.

Across the hall he could hear his mother's door opening. Shortly afterwards his door opened.

His mother sat down on the edge of his bed and placed her hand on his chest. She smiled, as she watched his chest rise and fall with each breath. "You know I love you, right?"

"Yeah, Mom. I love you, too."

"I know it's been a rough patch around here, but I didn't want you to forget that."

"I won't."

She took her hand off his chest and caressed his cheek. "You know, sometimes I look at you and I see your father. He was a good man."

Keith nodded. It had been a long time since she mentioned how much he resembled his father. He imagined it was probably a painful reminder of her loss at times.

"You're a good son." She leaned down and kissed his forehead.

"Thanks, Mom. You're a good mother."

She smiled and looked away. "If only that were true."

"But it is."

His mother stood and patted his arm. "I left a twenty on the counter. Use that to get yourself something for dinner. I have a meeting to go to tonight, and it will be a while before I get back."

"Okay."

"Make sure you lock up everything and set the alarm at ten."

"Sure. No problem."

Keith watched his mother walk away and then returned his gaze to the ceiling, losing himself in thoughts of Nakeisha and the future that lay ahead of them.

## CHAPTER FORTY-FOUR

KEITH WOKE AROUND MIDNIGHT. He quickly hopped out of bed when he realized he had not yet set the alarm for the house. The place was quiet and it was easy to tell that nothing had been disturbed. Still, he set the alarm. He didn't know why they even had an alarm. They lived in a small town where most people knew each other, especially the people on his street. He seriously doubted anyone would want to break into their house anyway. They had more books than anything else. If anyone was to get it in his head that he should break into the Lawrence household, he would be sorely disappointed. There was only one television in the house and it was an old 32-inch that wasn't even a flatscreen. They would need a cart to hall that thing off. And forget about HDMI cables and all of that stuff. This had only the coaxial cable nub and the crude audio/video ports. Keith didn't even have a video game console. To paraphrase Chris Tucker, if someone broke into the Lawrence household, they would just be practicing for a house that actually had something worth stealing.

When he finished punching in the alarm code, he

went to check his mother's bedroom. She was still out and about, and he wondered what his mother could have been doing after midnight. Did she have a man that she hadn't told him about? That would really be something, although he couldn't imagine his mother dating anyone; that was just this side of being what he would consider gross. Still, he wanted her to be happy regardless of what he thought. But after midnight? Mom had to be getting her freak on, he thought. He quickly shook his head, trying to rid himself of that image.

He walked back to his room and picked up his phone, checking to see if Nakeisha had called. No luck.

He checked his social media accounts, but quickly became bored. He had stopped caring about a lot of the stuff his classmates posted not long after he and Nakeisha had come from Pretty Tony's wake. His on-line presence by this point was purely obligational, just to make sure there wasn't something he was missing out on. He even felt guilty for being so weak that he couldn't function a day without being in the loop, even if he couldn't care less about what the loop was talking about.

He sat his phone down and lay back on his bed. So much had happened that day, but it was just the kind of thing you had to live with if you were a black resident of Daily. People liked to talk about how beautiful the town was and how idealistic it appeared, but those were people who didn't know much about the place, people who were stuck on the superficial.

At times, to Keith, it felt like there were two separate Dailys, one for whites and one for blacks. And the fact that he and Nakeisha lived on the integrated side of the railroad track, still two blocks from the white section of town, did not mean that their experience was any different from other blacks in the community. The only real difference was that the two of them were looking at using their educations to leave the town, whereas he suspected many of the black kids at the school would remain in Daily and rear their children there.

He had heard people say that the big cities intimidated them, but he preferred the idea of a big city and its opportunities to that of the claustrophobic passive-aggressive racism of Daily. Keith's mother had told him about the Great Migration, where hundreds of thousands of blacks left The South and moved north for better job opportunities. Decades later, Keith sympathized heavily. Sometimes he wished he could just disappear into the dark night.

When he finally did drift off to sleep, his mind still cloudy with thoughts of Daily, he entered one of the deepest, most dreamless sleeps of his young life.

# CHAPTER FORTY-FIVE

WHEN KEITH AWOKE the next morning, he found his mother stretched out across the sofa in the den, asleep. When she couldn't get to sleep in her own bed, she would spend the night there, her body pressed hard against the upper cushions. This, Keith imagined, was the closest she could get to reproducing the feel of his father's body lying next to her. He let her sleep.

After tiptoeing quietly through the house, he brushed his teeth, took his shower, and got dressed. He had no idea of what he would do that day, but he knew Nakeisha was an early riser and he wanted to be available to see her as soon as she called or texted him.

He hadn't heard from Nakeisha since the previous afternoon. He had hoped she would call last night, but she hadn't. He even went to sleep with his cell phone propped against his pillow just in case she wanted to say goodnight or something.

He considered calling her, but if he knew anything about Nakeisha in all the time he had known her, it was this: she did things in her own time. In fact, she struck him as one of the most deliberate people he knew. That was the reason he had confidence in the new direction their friendship had taken. In her personal life, Nakeisha only did things she wanted to do. He had yet to achieve the level of persuasiveness necessary to get her to act in any other way than her own.

With the *Monster Rising* compendium and Toni Morrison's *Song of Solomon* now complete, he considered driving over to the public library to look for something new to check out. He was unsure of what he wanted to read, but he had heard great things from Nakeisha about a novelist named Mat Johnson. The added bonus was that Mat Johnson wrote novels *and* graphic novels, which essentially covered all of Keith's interests. He wondered if the Daily Public Library carried any of Mat Johnson's books. He hoped they did.

He left his room and walked back to the den to check on his mother. She was still asleep, so he left a note for her on the counter in the kitchen.

The vehicles in the driveway were parked alongside each other like fraternal twins: the new hotness and the old rust bucket. The closer he got, the more he realized the vehicles were too closely parked. He wouldn't be able to get into his car because of how tightly his mother had parked. He reached in his pocket and took out his keys to open the driver side door to his mother's Jeep. That's when he noticed something odd. It looked as if a light bit of mud had brushed against the top of the door, just beneath the window. It was hardly noticeable, but because Keith knew his mother was very particular about her vehicle, he found it strange that she would drive through a puddle or whatever. Even stranger, he knew it hadn't rained in weeks, so maybe his mother had been driving and tried to throw away a soda or something and some droplets hit the vehicle. He licked his finger and wiped away the three small drops that rested right beneath the window. It didn't feel like mud or soda, but it didn't matter because he was more concerned about moving the Jeep enough so he could get into his own car and drive downtown.

Once he was able to get the Jeep over and away from his Jetta, he hopped down out of the driver seat and walked around to his car.

Then he saw it again. The dark droplets, only a few of them scattered along the maze of steel tubing making up the Jeep's grille guard, were barely noticeable. A person would have to stand at an angle to even notice them. He could also see specks of residue from what looked like soap.

The whole thing was strange. If he didn't know better, he would think that his mother might have actually hit a deer or something while she was out last night. He started to go back in the house and ask if she was okay, but she had seemed to be okay when he last left her snoring on the couch.

He hopped in his Jetta and headed over to the library without giving it another thought.

## CHAPTER FORTY-SIX

KEITH GOT the call from Nakeisha shortly before 11 that morning. She was breathless as she recounted what she had just heard about Brent Edwards. He was dead. They thought it was a hit and run out near the field on the backside of town. Even more, the person who did it was that white attorney who was running against Chante House for the District 44 senate seat. And the reason for all of this? It turns out that Brent Edwards, the starting quarterback and one of the most popular white guys in school, was actually black. Keith sat in his car, staring at the steering wheel. This was way too much for him to process. He wasn't close to Brent Edwards, but he knew him in passing. *Who didn't know Brent Edwards?*

Spooked by the strangeness of it all, Nakeisha asked him to come over, so he quickly drove home, parked his car, and walked down to her house.

"Oh my god," she said, opening the door and embracing him. "This is so crazy. It all feels so surreal."

"Yeah, I know," Keith said, his own mind racing with a million thoughts.

They both knew Daily was too small for the town

to be capable of talking about anything other than what they themselves were discussing.

It didn't take them very long to draw the connection between Pretty Tony and Brent Edwards. That Truelove guy who had run over Pretty Tony had committed a rare moment of racial violence, right? That's what they had assumed, but now, with this McKlusky guy, it felt like every adult white male wanted to kill a young black man. This idea scared the hell out of Keith, but he didn't want to let Nakeisha know just how much.

"He's in jail, right?" Keith asked.

"From what I hear. And get this: his daughter—you know Heidi McKlusky—she is the one who dropped the dime on him to the cops."

"Man," Keith said, sighing. "That's crazy." In the back of his mind, though, he was thankful that the McKlusky guy was still in police custody. He would be unable to sleep knowing the person who killed Brent Edwards was still out and about roaming the streets.

"I swear I can't move away from this place fast enough," Nakeisha said. "People here are crazy."

Keith could only nod. He knew that she would in fact leave as soon as she could, but he dreaded that day because he knew that would be the day that they were officially over—at least in the only way he knew them to be.

"What does this mean for the election?" he asked, suddenly aware that this situation had unintended consequences that might possibly work in their favor.

"I guess Chante House will win by default. Kind of like winning on a forfeit."

"That's a good thing, right?" Keith said.

Nakeisha shook her head. "I don't think, in the

whole scheme of things, anyone can win in a situation like this."

"But Chante's one of the good guys. That has to mean something."

"I don't know." Nakeisha shrugged, her eyes distant and dazed. "Maybe." She scrunched up her face as she pondered it. "What I don't understand is how that guy knew Brent was black. I swear I have seen Brent Edwards a million times over the past few years, and I never once looked at him and thought he was anything other than white."

"I thought he was white, too. My mother told me that, back in the day, they thought some guy named Homer Plessy was white, and he was only 1/8 black. He got arrested for sitting in the white section of a train. If the railroad company hadn't gotten wind of what he was trying to do, they might've thought he was white and let him go about his business. There was a whole Supreme Court case about it. I think that's where 'separate but equal' came from."

Nakeisha nodded. "Yeah. We read about that in history class. But that was back in the late 1800s. This is 2014!"

"I know," Keith responded, digesting the severity of it all.

"First Pretty Tony. Now Brent. Now I'm scared for you, Keith."

"I'm cool. No one is out to get me," he said, feigning the courage he so desperately wanted.

"I hope not. I couldn't take it if anything happened to you," Nakeisha said.

Keith started to respond, "Neither could I," but he only nodded.

Nakeisha stood and stretched her thin frame. "Can I tell you something weird?"

"Sure."

"When I first heard that Brent Edwards got hit by a car, the first thing I thought was that it was retaliation for Pretty Tony. But when I heard that Brent was black, too, that idea didn't make a lot of sense."

As Keith listened to Nakeisha, he felt as though his stomach were being blown out by a shotgun.

The Grand Cherokee in the driveway and those mysterious droplets.

The pictures of the lynchings.

*Song of Solomon.*

In *Song of Solomon* there was a group called the Seven Days, and their primary existence was built around recreating atrocities committed on black people by committing them on random white people. Is that what happened here? Was his mother involved in any of this? His mind filled up so quickly that he could only feel himself shaking with fear.

"Are you okay?" Nakeisha asked.

"I need to go."

"Keith, what's wrong?"

"I just need a minute."

"But Keith—"

"Keisha, I need a minute. Can you please just give a minute? Damn."

She backed away from him, visibly upset, but he couldn't allow himself to worry about that. He had to go home and talk to his mother. And if she was still asleep, he would wake her.

## CHAPTER FORTY-SEVEN

KEITH FOUND his mother in her office, seated at her computer.

"Why, Mom?" he said, closing the door behind him.

"What?"

"Why did you kill him?"

His mother rose from her seat so quickly she was a blur. She placed her hand over his mouth and pushed him against the door.

"Don't say that!" she said, her eyes thick with water.

Keith was shocked. He had expected his mother to deny his accusation by acting as if she didn't know what he was talking about. He hadn't expected her to charge him.

"Listen, Keith, baby. You don't know what you're talking about." She slowly removed her hand from his mouth. "Sit down. We need to talk."

Keith looked at his mother, and for the first time in his life, he actually feared her. It was as if he didn't know her at all. He sat down, staring at her, unable to look away.

"They have been killing us for centuries, Keith. They have shot us, hung us, disfigured, dismembered, burned, drowned, castrated, raped, and then taken pieces of us for souvenirs. They have murdered us on courthouse lawns while their little children watched. They are evil."

"Who, Mom?"

"Boy, I know I raised you to be smarter than this. White people, Keith! White people!"

"But that boy—Brent Edwards—he was black!"

"No, he wasn't, Keith. He was white."

"No, Mom, he was *black*. He was adopted," Keith said, repeating what Nakeisha had told him.

"He was white."

"Mom."

"Keith, he was white, okay?"

His mother was now in tears, although there was an emptiness there, too.

She had all but confessed that it had been her who had killed Brent Edwards, and the two of them crying hysterically in her small office would not change that.

When Keith was able to collect his breath, he said, "The McKlusky guy. They arrested him for what happened."

"Yeah," his mother responded. "They did. I didn't tell his daughter to turn him in."

"But aren't you going to tell the truth?"

"Keith," she said, wiping her eyes, "the truth is that these white people murdered your father."

"But you said he was killed in a car accident."

"They ran him off the road. A group of white teenagers. They saw him, and they thought it would be fun if they ran a black man off the road."

"What did the police do to the white guys?"

"Nothing. Those crackers claimed they saw him fall asleep behind the wheel and drive off the road."

"How do you know that's not what happened?"

"Trust me. I just know."

"Oh Mom," Keith said. He grabbed her and held her close to him. He didn't know whether to believe her or not. He was afraid not to. After all, the alternative was that his mother had simply snapped.

They would come and arrest her, and he would finish high school an orphan. She wasn't much of a mother to him, but she was all he had. He didn't know if he could let them take her away.

For a while the two of them sat in the office trying not to look at each other, his mother in her own incomprehensible thoughts, he in his own.

Finally, Keith stood. "Mom, let's go."

"You're turning me in," she said, resignedly.

"No, Mom. We need to do a better job of washing your car."

KEITH UNFOLDED the sheet of paper, pressing his palms across it to smooth it down. Even from the distance of his nose to the desk, he could smell Nakeisha's scent.

He stared at the letter for a long moment before lifting it slightly and finally reading it.

*Dear Keith,*

*I know this is so old school, writing you this letter when I could have just texted you, but I always liked the idea of you going to your mailbox and receiving an actual letter from me. So here it is! :-)*

*I have been at a summer program here at Hampton University for a week now, and being away from Daily has given me a chance to really think about things. I know this hasn't been an easy year for you, and I have often wondered what happened to change the way we were last summer, but I figure you will tell me when you're ready.*

*Guess who made a donation to my summer program tuition? Senator Chante House! It turns out she's a Hampton University alum. She is so my shero! I'm so glad she got elected! I hear she's doing great things down in Jackson. She even offered me a job at her Daily office after school this coming school year. Maybe I can take you out with my first paycheck, that is if you're cool with that.*

*Ever since they acquitted that McKlusky guy of murder, I have been worried for your safety. The fact that they let him go is just another example of white justice in The South. I heard someone say that he moved away with some black woman, but I know that's just some made-up stuff. No black woman in her right mind would be caught dead with a man like him. I hope that he is gone, though. That way he can't ever hurt you.*

*I miss you. I guess that's all I'm really trying to say. I miss you—and I miss us. I hope that we can make this last year at Daily High count.*

*Give my best to your mother.*

*Love you much!!!*

*Keisha*

He reached for a notebook on his desk, opened it, and grabbed a pen. He stared at the blank page, his mind full of all of the things he wanted to tell her. He rested the nib of the pen gently on the paper, his hand aching with anticipation. He wanted to tell her the truth about everything, about his mother and his own role in covering things up. He also wanted to tell her that he loved her, too, that despite all that had happened, maybe they could still be happy together.

He wanted to tell her all of these things, but his fingers would not grant him the freedom to do so. His self-imposed sentence would not allow him to compose a single sentence, even if that sentence could have saved him.

Instead, he set his pen down and returned the letter to its envelope, placing it in the back of his notebook.

He arose from his desk and walked out into the sweltering summer air, feeling his dreams of escaping Daily, Mississippi, ignite into flames all around him.

He suspected that the ashes of those dreams would get pressed deep into the earth, alongside the red clay, encasing themselves in the tomb of his memories.

It was then that he remembered the poem "Harlem" by Langston Hughes. The question of what happened to a dream deferred now had an answer. With sweat streaming down his face, the air a furnace scraping at his skin in waves, Keith knew that sometimes dreams really did just explode.

## ACKNOWLEDGMENTS

I would like to thank my father, Randolph Walker, Sr.; the late Senator Bennie L. Turner; my brother, Torrey; my mother, Jeanne Walker; my loving wife, Lauren; and my beautiful daughter, Zoë. Without them, this book would not have been possible.

# ALSO BY RAN WALKER

# ABOUT THE AUTHOR

Ran Walker is the winner of the 2019 National Indie Author of the Year Award (selected by judges from Library Journal, Publisher's Weekly, IngramSpark, St. Martin's Press, and Writer's Digest), the 2019 Black Caucus of the American Library Association Best Fiction Ebook Award, and the 2018 Virginia Indie Author Project Award for Adult Fiction. He is also the recipient of both a 2005 Mississippi Arts Commission/NEA artist grant and a 2006 artist mini-grant. He served as an Artist-in-Residence with the Mississippi Arts Commission in 2006. Additionally, he is a past participant in the Hurston-Wright Writers Week Workshop and is the recipient of a fellowship from the Callaloo Writers Workshop. He teaches creative writing at Hampton University and lives in Virginia with his wife and daughter.

www.ingramcontent.com/pod-product-compliance
Lightning Source LLC
Chambersburg PA
CBHW061035120726
47910CB00006B/2260